"A shipwreck on a haunted island…creepy, suspenseful, and chilling! A real page-turner of blood, guts, and ghouls."

—Sèphera Girón, author of *Captured Souls*

"*INFERNAL* is an exciting horror story with a terrifying twist!"

—Amber Fallon, author of *Terminal* and *The Warblers*

"That burning Lovecraftian quest for knowledge, that incendiary drive that propels Science, Religion, and Metaphysics, impels a diverse group of adventurers to explore an island and an ocean avoided by indigenous mainlanders. What they discover is marine and island life amazing in size and nature; but they also discover the converse of the Lovecraftian Coin: the Knowledge we uncover may drive us to Madness."

—The Haunted Reading Room

"Sustained suspense and masterful writing guide the reader through a very dark adventure. Stakes are raised, shocks are bloody, and the horror chilling. The cumulative effect is absolutely apocalyptic."

—Stuart R. West, author of *Ghosts of Gannaway* and *Twisted Tales from Tornado Alley*

INFERNAL

INFERNAL

Cheryl Low

A
Grinning Skull Press
Publication
PO Box 67, Bridgewater, MA 02324

The Skull logo with stylized lettering was created for Grinning Skull Press by Dan Moran, http://dan-moran-art.com/.
Cover designed by Jeffrey Kosh, http://jeffreykosh.wix.com/jeffreykoshgraphics.

ISBN: 1-947227-17-3 (paperback)
ISBN-13: 978-1-947227-17-0 (paperback)
ISBN: 978-1-947227-18-7 (ebook)

DEDICATION

To my horror movie partner, Phong Chau, for never trying to scare me
even though we live together and there have been so many
opportunities.

Contents

ACKNOWLEDGMENTS

This project owes thanks to Whitley and Leaf for being such amazing sounding boards.

And to my mother-in-law, Anh Dao Tang, for her support and kindred love of scary stories.

The ground rumbled. The ocean stirred.
And the land did break, decisive in its wisdom to cut
away a great evil.
To cripple its reach and make a prison of sand and trees.
Waves became the walls that held back the first monster.
Saving all others from its ceaseless hunger.

Prologue

The sailor ran toward the sound of the ocean, stumbling blindly through the midnight jungle. Mammals, birds, and insects screamed and chirped, calling out into the night as though to mask the sound of waves—working with the nightmare of this island to keep him forever lost inside a prison of foliage and teeth.

Only days ago they'd thought this island a blessing, gifted to them in the aftermath of a storm and the sinking of their ship.

They had been wrong—and now he was the only one left. The jungle had claimed the others, one by one. Blood plastered his clothes to his chest, sticking to his hands, but it wasn't his.

His boot caught on some vicious, overgrown root of the jungle floor, casting him forward onto his belly just as he broke free of the trees and vines. For a moment he didn't move to rise, panting against the coarse sand and listening to the waves. They called him, beckoning him to the only escape left.

He lifted his head, and under the bright moon, he saw the shimmering ocean, beautiful with her offer of certain death. He crawled to her, clawing and kicking at the sand in a frantic race to the foam gathering at the edge of her surf.

The ravenous jungle behind him went quiet, and that silence stabbed at his heart, bringing tears to his eyes. "It will not be me. It will not be me."

He stretched, desperate for the waves. "You will not take me."

His body jerked to a stop, fingers curling back just as the water would have reached him.

A violent breath sucked deep into his chest, burning through his lungs, his muscles, his soul—leaving nothing behind but a body sitting on the beach, smiling at the moon.

With a sigh, he stood. The waves crashed and rolled with new anger, reaching for him, always reaching. The man, no longer himself, took a step back, and then another, until he disappeared into the shadows of his jungle once more.

Chapter 1

As a child, Valarie DeNola would jump right into the deep end of the pool. She wouldn't dip her toes or wade in slowly on the steps of the shallow end. She wouldn't even look into the water before leaping. She just shed her towel and her mother's hand and ran full force to the edge, jumping high and falling hard into the deep. That never changed. Not even when she traded a pool for the ocean.

* * *

To say there is no sound underwater isn't true. The press against her eardrums, the beating of her pulse, and the shifting of her suit was sound all its own—blocking out any chance of quiet. But sound was different below water than above, contained by her skull and echoing from her body.

Val held onto the bar of her cage and stared out into the deep. She loved this moment, the one when waiting became almost unbearable. Bits of fish gore fluttered through the water from the boat above. The passengers were chumming while she and the other divers waited. It wasn't difficult to find predators in these waters, and experience had taught Val that it wouldn't take long. Through goggles she watched, straining to make out moving shapes, darker blues drifting closer. The excitement clogged her throat, fingers gripping the cage as that body swam closer and closer, unable to tell size and distance until it was finally clear within sight and still so large.

Her earpiece crackled when the crew on deck saw the shark from their perch. "Incoming," Jessie said excitedly.

Val reached out to the side to grab onto Terrance's shoulder. He'd been fidgety in the cage the past few days, but he was getting better. He held onto his camera with both hands, body turning toward the viewing frame in the bars. But he didn't face it just because it offered the best view. It was where he would feel the most vulnerable, and that camera in his hands became the last barrier between himself and whatever came up from the deep. Terrance learned quickly, even if it was his first season in the water with them. Felix liked him, but no one was surprised there. Her husband could befriend a feral baboon if given some time and a bottle of tequila.

Val looked to the second shark cage dangling there in the open water, bobbing with large, black floaties breaking the surface overhead. Felix and another videographer were there to mirror them in their wetsuits and dive gear.

The shark came in close, swimming between the two cages to take a look at the boat before circling Felix. "Anyone we know?" Val asked, watching him study the massive fish. It was at least sixteen feet and female. If they didn't know her, they should. They had been coming to this spot to observe the great whites for the last four years. Val could see the bright yellow tag on the dorsal fin from where she bobbed in her own cage.

"Looks like Mimi," Felix replied in her left ear, his thick Spanish accent familiar and always comforting.

Val shifted in the cage to trade sides with Terrance, making sure he had the best shots he could get. Usually, she would have a camera herself, but with the new show they were filming, they agreed to take on more camera crew and get her into some of the shots for once.

For the past six years, it had been Felix on the screen and Val holding the camera. She used to tell him what he was looking at, what kinds of fish they were, and what was normal or abnormal about them, but Felix learned fast; she never had to tell him anything twice.

She had expected Felix to get bored with the ocean eventually, the way he'd gotten bored with skydiving, helicopter flying, mountain climbing, and extreme camping before they met. But she had been wrong. Something about the ocean captivated him the way it did her. They could go to the same spots every year to see the same sharks, and somehow it never got old.

"We have two more, Val," Felix said over the comm system. Excitement rang in his voice, inciting it in everyone who heard him.

The cage rocked, and Val snapped her head to the side to see the large body of a male great white push past. Terrance bumped into her, and she braced his side to keep him steady while he filmed. She was sure he'd get the hang of this job—eventually.

The shark rushed up to the surface toward the boat, attacking the chum as though it might make a run for it.

The third shark rolled by in the wake of the male, swimming right by the cage to eye them. For one sickly moment, Val worried it would whip its head right through that gap of steel bars. It wouldn't fit, she was positive, but that didn't stop her stomach from lifting up into her throat when it looked back at her, seeming to hear her thoughts. When that big, black eye looked away, she noticed the pattern of scars along the head of the shark and the old scar on her pectoral fin.

"Kajsa," Val breathed. She'd named the shark after a mountain in Sweden that she had climbed with her sister after graduation. Val still had another year of schooling left at the time and no idea that it would lead her to the ocean years later, filming sharks with her husband and a team of fanatics and camera jockeys.

They'd tagged Kajsa on their first trip to this spot and took notice of her every season since. She was big, and she knew it. She liked to push the cages around. Last year she'd even gnawed one of the floaties to pieces. Felix loved her because unpredictable sharks made for thrilling footage and exciting dives. Val wasn't as enthusiastic about the big brute.

"I was wondering when we'd see her." Felix laughed over the comm, and it crackled in her ear.

Val watched the shark drift away, back down into the dark. Her heartbeat picked up the moment she lost sight of Kajsa, but by then the male had circled around and was bumping Felix's cage, giving the other cage a close encounter and Terrance some great footage.

For a few more minutes, everything went smoothly. Just enough excitement to keep everyone laughing and grinning on adrenaline. A chill ran up her spine, making her shake out her shoulders and turn her head to the side, expecting to see something stalking her in the deep. Instead, she saw Felix in his cage across the blue. Everything was a sort of slow-motion underwater. She exhaled, and bubbles rolled up toward the surface.

And then Kajsa hit her cage full force. Not from the side, but from the bottom. Slamming hard against the gate at their feet and pushing with such force that the whole thing launched upward. The cage broke the surface, and for a horrible second, gravity was upon them, pulling Val and Terrance against the bars. The bright morning sun glared down at them before the cage tipped forward.

Val slammed against the bars of the half wall, grabbing at them to hang on when the floaties smacked against the surface of the ocean. She expected the cage to swing back down into the usual upright position, but Kajsa was still under them. Still pushing. Still thrashing.

Val couldn't hear anything when everyone started shouting over the comm system at the same time. Their voices became a tangled mess that blared through the earpiece to rival her own pulse. With that massive, toothed fish beneath, she couldn't be sure if she was even breathing. Her fingers clutched so tightly at the bars that the bones in her arms strained and shook. Her legs kicked, trying to pull up under herself for fear of popping out of the cage through the viewing hole now beneath her.

Somewhere in the flurry of sounds and panic, she heard Felix's voice shouting "babe" in that sharp tone he always said that particular pet name in. It was something he said when she was close to danger—or in this case, teeth. It wasn't creative or cute or even all that endearing, like the plethora of nicknames he'd made up for her over the years. It was the tone and the word he used when he was afraid, and it set her nerves on fire. She sucked in a breath that made her lungs ache to scream or curse.

She had forgotten Terrance entirely until his camera sunk into the blue in her line of sight. It had fallen out of the cage through the large viewing frame set in the bars. She tasted bile when Terrance sank into the deep after it.

For a sickly half-second, Val clung to the bars, leaning out that gap in the cage. She stared past the thrashing of Kajsa's tail and the glint of teeth, through the bubbles of the foaming surface at Terrance's body sinking, falling. His arms stretched to grab at the camera he'd dropped before he twisted around entirely to look up at her, up at the cage he was no longer tucked inside of, and up at the great white violently attacking the metal that was the only promise of safety. He let the camera fall, kicking weakly to keep himself from sinking farther but with nowhere to go.

Val watched another shadow of a shark roll through the darker water beneath him, circling the scene.

She let go of the bars and slipped out of the cage, diving down after Terrance, and heard Felix shouting through the earpiece. He wasn't speaking English anymore, but she recognized the Spanish as a flurry of curses and prayers all merged into one big sacrilegious plea. She kicked the cage to launch herself out and down just as Kajsa abandoned her metal prey, bumping it one last time before swimming off to circle around.

When Kajsa moved away, the curious male shark returned, teeth bared and moving right for Terrance. Val kicked harder, heart slamming in her chest as she swam toward the scene. The shark grew larger the closer it swam, and just before she reached Terrance, she saw that black eye roll back and vanish. She grabbed onto his arm and pulled hard enough that, had this been any other situation, she might have worried about his shoulder.

Terrance bumped into her, and the shark bumped into him, pushing them roughly to the side and spinning them both. Val caught a glimpse of their cage, empty and right-side up. And beyond it, she saw the second cage with Felix and the other cameraman, Gary, fighting. He was probably trying to keep Felix in the cage.

The comm system continued to crackle violently with too many voices. The captain on deck called her name repeatedly. Gary tried to give updates to the boat about what was going on while grappling with Felix. Felix cursed a lot of people and tried to get out into the open water.

Val pushed Terrance up, ahead of herself and back toward their cage. The swim felt like a sprint, her heart pounding and her muscles burning. From the corner of her eye, Val saw another shark. She twisted when it came too close, hand stretching out to push her gloved palm against the nose, above all those teeth. She locked her elbow and kept her arm straight. Shoving hard, she pushed herself to the side.

As soon as the shark passed, Val started kicking again, swimming for the cage. When she saw Terrance climbing inside, she felt a wash of relief and maybe even disbelief. They'd actually survived. It was going to be a great story. It was going to make for great footage if Gary managed to get any of it.

Val was so close to the cage. So close to this being one of those great *close calls*.

She almost didn't see Kajsa coming from underneath. Her white belly gleamed when it reached the stretches of light and gave her away in that last second.

She heard Felix shout. Not "babe" like when he was worried or afraid, but this time it was her name. Her whole name. And it sounded like the last time she would ever hear it.

Kajsa struck her from beneath, and all Val felt was the slam of the shark's weight against her. She didn't feel teeth. The brutal force of the shark's body drove her to the surface. For one horrible moment, Val was airborne but not alone. The sky shone blue, and the sun glared brightly. The water flailed through the air by Kajsa's lashing tail, droplets glimmering like stars.

The giant shark twisted in the air and came down with Val.

And then she was alone.

She couldn't move. She wasn't even sure she was breathing. She bobbed just below the surface, looking down at the deep and at Kajsa's disappearing shadow. The shark drifted deeper and deeper, farther away from Val, and all she could wonder was, why? Why would she leave when she finally had her? All those years of watching each other. All those years of Kajsa studying their cages and getting closer and closer. She finally had Val, stunned and drifting like deadwood in the sea, and she swam away.

Val slowly started sinking, drawn downward like debris. She told herself to kick, to move, to lift her head and find the boat, but she couldn't.

A cloud of red gathered around her, wispy at the edges where it faded into the blue but sickly thick all around her body. She watched that red until the sun blinded her. Her back landed on the surface of the boat, and she finally felt the weight of gravity bearing down on her. Felix pulled off her mask and held her face in his hands. His palms were so warm against her cheeks. He said that she was going to be okay over and over again. Val wanted to nod, but she couldn't. When he had to let go of her to do something else, she turned her head to the side and saw how much thicker that red looked splattering the deck.

"You're going to be okay," Felix said again, cupping her cheek to turn her head up so that she could only see him and the sky.

Val watched him until she lost consciousness, but even when she blacked out, she could still hear the waves smacking against the sides of the boat. She still heard the waves in the hospital, and sometimes now, years later, when she closes her eyes, no matter how far inland she might be, she still hears those waves.

Chapter 2

More than three years later, and not for the first time by a long shot, Val was on another boat in the ocean. She watched the sun come up over the blue horizon rather than looking at the island behind her. They weren't far from land, but she was more than happy to stay on the boat. The sky changed colors over the sea. She'd seen it happen at least a thousand times, the dark shades of night giving way in slow folds to light through waves of pink and orange. It never got old.

The coffee cup in her right hand passed to the left, sharing warmth between palms and digits. Kajsa had taken a chunk out of her left hand, leaving Val with three fingers and a thumb but no pinky and a particularly ugly scar trailing up her forearm. Sometimes, when changing, she took a moment to bend her arm in just the right way so that the scars lined up over her hand, forearm, upper arm, and back. All those teeth, like razors through her skin, and yet somehow the shark only took a pinky. Kajsa managed to break a number of bones and tear a lot of flesh. Even after they healed, the bruises gone and the stitches removed, the scars still looked gruesome—thick, puckered flesh in pale, jagged lines twisting around her body.

She heard Julie practically skip onto deck behind her, deeply breathing the ocean air as though for the first time. Val took another drink of coffee to hide her amusement. Even when they were kids, Julie had been a morning person. Up at dawn and happy about it. Val, on the other hand, reserved all enthusiasm for after eight.

Julie bumped into her on purpose and then promptly stole the mug from her hands. She wore a blue cable knit sweater and had her brown hair in a messy bun. When they were kids, they looked nothing alike—different noses, different heights—and yet, somehow it had all evened out over the years. On more than one occasion, Julie and Valarie convinced friends that they were twins in college.

Val pushed up the sleeves of her hoodie just as the sun finally peeked over the horizon to spread out over the surface of the water. She could hear the crew stirring down below and a particularly large grumble about creamer that had to have been Julie's fiancé, Zach. They had met in the rainforests of Peru. Julie had been there with a group of other biologists to look for new species and take samples while Zach had been there as a wildlife photographer. Love at first sight, it seemed, or, as Val liked to say, *love at first bug bite.*

Julie had dragged Val into the rainforest once, and that had been enough. She'd only managed to get her along on this trip by promising that Val wouldn't have to step foot on the island. She'd even made Julie write it into her contract with the channel they were filming for just so there couldn't be any misunderstandings.

Val turned to look at her sister. The shadowy peak of Isla de los Perdidos loomed in the still-dark sky behind her.

It wasn't much. A speck of land coated in thick vegetation and humming with life, relatively untouched. A handful of attempts to make settlements on it over the last five hundred years had been unsuccessful, and the locals on the mainland offered only ghost stories for explanations.

Isla de los Perdidos was abandoned. An island within eyesight of the continent it had broken away from centuries ago and yet completely uninhabited by people. The locals wouldn't even go there to show Julie and her team around. It had all just made her more excited about the idea of spending a week on it. Julie wanted to know all of its secrets, possibly discover something new, and then show the world. She and Zach were taking two videographers, Henry and Megan, with them. Julie had worked with them in Cameroon and boasted their skills to the company.

Val got the chance to meet them the night before when they arrived at the mainland, before boarding the Charlene, a boat she had worked on before with its captain, Kevin Lochner. She was close friends with his husband, Calvin, and had worked with him dozens of times on dives for different programs. They did tropical work along reefs and beaches in Central and South America.

"Sleep well?" Val asked her sister, knowing the answer.

"Not a wink!" Julie was too excited. She was like that, too much energy for her own good sometimes—though most of the time that energy and excitement worked in her favor.

Julie spent the last eighteen months getting together this expedition and its funding. She'd worked it out so there would be three teams with camera crews to get the most material possible for the videographers, and thus the nature channel to which Julie had pitched this whole expedition. Julie, Zach, Henry, and Megan would go to the island to unravel its mysteries. Calvin, an experienced diver and cameraman, would go with Oliver Camden, a salvager, and Maeko Watanabe, a marine biologist particularly beloved by the channel, to take a look at the reef.

At least a dozen ships had sunk in these waters, and Julie had convinced Oliver that he might find something worthwhile. Oliver was a bit of a prick but good at his job and excited to go hunting for sunken ships.

Julie gave Val back her coffee after drinking half of it and then complaining about how much sugar was in it. Val gave her a vaguely sympathetic look. She knew what she was getting when she took it.

"So, when are you setting off?" Val asked, and Julie beamed with excitement. Val took another sip of her now-cold coffee to hide the way her sister's smile infected her own mouth.

Henry and Megan, each carrying a camera and bouncing bags of lenses and supplies on their hips, were arguing about something as they made their way up from below deck. They looked almost as eager as her sister.

Julie glanced back at them before looking at Val again, and then past her shoulder to the ocean. Val didn't think her sister was looking at anything in particular until she got that look that triggered her flashbacks from their childhood. She half expected Bobby Spencer from sixth grade to be sneaking up on her with a spider.

"We're just going to get some interviews of the teams and make sure everyone is settled in before we head out for the island," Julie said, forgetting to breathe between words, and Val knew in that instant her sister was hiding something.

Val frowned because Julie looked outright guilty. Was Bobby Spencer really emerging from the ocean behind her? Val turned her head to look back over her shoulder and squinted at the small boat making its way toward them, cutting a line from the horizon. "What do you mean settled in? We're already settled," she mumbled.

Julie took her coffee again, and Val looked at her, noting that she didn't drink it this time. She just held onto it. Was she afraid she would throw it?

"Okay. So, you know how much the network loves him," Julie started in that casual tone, the diplomatic yet somehow flippant one she liked to take up when she knew she was in trouble but had no intention of apologizing.

Val stared at her for an awkward length of time before sucking a breath and realizing what her sister had done. "No," she exhaled, then turned to look at the approaching boat again. It was much worse than some shitty eleven-year-old boy and a bug. It was her ex-husband.

"He gets great ratings, and the network just loved the idea of seeing the two of you working together again. They're talking about it being the feature of next year's summer programming!" She pitched her sentences with shrill enthusiasm now. It earned her Henry's attention, the young cameraman making his way closer to discreetly film their interaction.

Val let out a groan and grabbed her coffee cup from her sister. Julie looked worried about the tacky green porcelain, but Val didn't throw it at anyone just yet. "I need more coffee," she mumbled, and shouldered past Julie.

Her sister heaved a whine and turned to watch her retreat. "It's mostly sugar!" she shouted after her.

"Then I need more sugar!" Val called back. Megan almost bumped into her but quickly skirted to the side, looking sheepish. She could hear Julie already recovering from their interaction to tell Henry that they could get started with the crew interviews. She would go first. Julie never shied away from being the leader. It was a great quality. It's too bad she didn't shy away from stabbing people in the back either.

Val felt abruptly trapped when she reached the little kitchen below deck. She filled her cup halfway and then started heaping in spoonfuls of sugar.

Calvin came in just in time to watch the last two spoonfuls go in and raised an eyebrow. "Looking for some diabetes to go with that sulk?" he asked, taking two mugs from the cupboard, one metal and the other chipped and stained but bearing the name "Lochner" written across its front in permanent marker. He filled both mugs with black coffee and left it at that. Neither Calvin nor his husband were fans of sugar or milk in their coffee. Val remembered from the last few times she went out to sea with them. They both enjoyed giving her a hard time when it came to her sugar intake. Calvin liked things sour, and Lochner was the classic ship's captain—he only overindulged in black coffee, facial hair, and ugly sweaters.

They were an odd pair, even at sea. Calvin was clean shaven, organized, and stylish. He had a collection of vintage t-shirts and sunglasses that Val realized after their third outing together must be extensive because she never saw him in the same ones twice. His diving gear and cameras were always meticulously cared for, and he did sets of sit-ups and push-ups every morning. She'd witnessed it a number of times and seen the results in the form of hard abs and cut traps.

Calvin was fit, and he was the kind of bastard that walked around like he didn't know it. Val, of course, didn't mind because, aside from being pleasant to look at, Calvin was a smug, funny, cocky sort of person who did amazing work filming in the water.

Lochner, on the other hand, she had never once seen off his boat. Not even in the water. In fact, Val was fairly certain she had never even seen him out of a thick sweater. He was a big man with large brown eyes and a beard that was very close to being too much. He wore a knitted ski cap all of the time, but Val could vaguely remember seeing sun-bleached curls sticking out from under it once before. While Calvin could talk for hours, Lochner kept his sentences short and rare. It insured that, when he did give a command, it got attention.

She supposed they were a lot like their mugs. Different, but both on this ship, day after day, traveling the oceans like it was all home to them.

Val looked Calvin in the eye and put another spoonful of sugar in her cup before defiantly stirring it into a thick sludge.

He smiled, sunglasses clipped to the collar of today's t-shirt—vintage X-men. "Found out about the ex coming aboard, did you?"

Val frowned deeper.

Calvin shrugged and picked up his coffees. "All passengers had to be cleared with Loch," he explained his know-how and turned away from her, heading toward the narrow stairs that led above deck.

"You could have warned me." She was sure he was still smiling.

"Could have," he agreed and then disappeared, an expert at carrying multiple full cups up the stairs of a swaying ship.

Val leaned her hip into the linoleum-coated counter and took a sip of her sweet fuel. She could hear the voices above deck. Henry had caught sight of Calvin on his way up and tried to stop him for an interview, but based on the awkward way his words dropped off, Calvin hadn't stopped in his route to the wheelhouse.

She took another sip, wondering already what she was supposed to tell those cameras. The same old stuff, she guessed. Who she was, where they were, what they were there to do, and why her. Why her was a good question. She smiled and put the lip of her mug to her mouth again. The answers were always the same. It was her job to be here because she knew the ocean and the things living in it. She was also here because her sister was the one obsessed with the island and couldn't have gathered the funding for an island expedition that may turn up nothing unless she'd promised the sure bet of shark footage for the channel. Most of all, Valarie DeNola was here because she was the fool willing to get into the water every time they gave her a chance.

One of the cabin doors opened, and Oliver Camden walked out. His short coppery hair stuck out on one side, and his skin was shaded in deep tans, hinting at the shapes of shirts he wore when sunburned. Despite bedhead, he appeared bright-eyed and ready for the day. In fact, he looked like he'd been up for a while—freshly shaven and dumping an armful of maps, rulers, pens, and a tablet onto the communal table. Val frowned because she was pretty sure he wasn't going to move that shit anytime soon by the way he immediately started spreading it all out and used cups for weights at the corners of maps.

She took another deep swallow of caffeine and sugar and watched him. He didn't look her way or say anything to acknowledge her. At least three minutes of silence stretched out between them while Val stared at his profile, trying to decide if she was being ignored or if he was just oblivious.

At last, he looked up. But not at her. Oliver swiveled around in the tight space and noticed for the first time that something was missing.

He marched three steps and pounded his fist against a narrow cabin door. "Maeko!" he shouted through the thin wood. A grumbling came from inside. "Get the fuck up, girl!" he hollered, Irish accent thick. "I'll leave you behind if you're not ready to go in an hour." His eagerness looked greedy, and he hadn't even gotten into the water yet. Val already hated the idea of him actually finding anything worthwhile but was also pretty sure he'd make for a great show. Cameras love douchebags.

Maeko Watanabe practically stumbled out of her cabin, scrubbing her face to try to convince herself she was awake.

"Coffee?" Val suggested.

Maeko scrunched her face as though offended by the idea, but shuffled closer, drawn by the gravitation of caffeine. She pushed up the long sleeves of her tight shirt and clawed fingers through her long black hair, dragging the mess back from her pale face and binding it with one of the hair ties around her wrist.

Val scooted to the side to let the shorter woman by. She fumbled for a mug, eyes still blinking a little too slowly. Val tried not to smile.

"Get me a cup," Oliver said in that casual way, completely certain one of them would do it. Val stood there long enough to see that Maeko pretended successfully not to have heard him, filling her own cup and drinking it on her way to the bathroom.

Oliver looked up from his maps when he realized he still didn't have his coffee, and for the first time that morning, his blue eyes landed on Val. She did smile then and took a sip from her cup before turning away from him. It was going to be a long week. She climbed the narrow stairs back into the rising daylight while he grumbled a curse and got his own coffee.

Chapter 3

A sleek speedboat was bound to the side of the Charlene and being emptied. Julie helped Felix unload supplies while Megan followed them with a camera, asking questions while they worked. Val decided not to notice Felix just yet, stopping beside Henry and smiling at Poppy. The shark enthusiast was currently beaming for Henry's camera and talking about how she'd discovered her love of danger.

Val had heard the story a dozen times before. She and Felix had still been together back when they found Poppy. She'd been a surfer in the waves of South Africa, more interested in the sharks that broke the surface than in the waters themselves. Poppy had contacted them, looking to work on their boat for the season. She'd been on deck the day Kajsa hit Val. She'd expected it to scare Poppy out of the lifestyle, but, as she eventually came to realize, nothing scared Poppy.

When the young woman took her large brown eyes from the camera long enough to notice Val standing there, she shot up from her seat. She was tall and lean, nothing but muscles. Her dark skin soaked up the sunlight she swam in every day but never managed to hide the beautiful splay of freckles across her nose and cheeks, matching the ones down her shoulders.

"Valentine!" she screamed, and Val cringed at the nickname she'd never okayed. The younger woman launched herself forward and hugged Val, squeezing tight. "I'm so excited we're working together!" She was still yelling even though her mouth was close to Val's ear. "What the hell have you been up to? I heard you've been filming crocodiles." Poppy leaned back to look at her but didn't entirely let her go. She scrunched her face at the idea of reptiles, but Val could already see a glimmer of interest in those eyes.

Henry jumped up from where he'd been sitting, still holding the camera anchored on his shoulder but turning to have both women in the shot. "Crocodiles? I thought you only did ocean work?"

Poppy moved to the side and stole Val's mug from her fingers. She drank from the stolen cup and didn't seem at all surprised by the amount of sugar in the usually bitter brew.

Val cleared her throat and shrugged a little. She'd always felt a little awkward being on this side of the camera. "Um, well, these were crocs in the ocean off Australia. But I did do some camera work on land, up rivers. I'm a marine biologist, so it's kind of a waste if I'm not in the water." She smiled a little. "At least, I think it's a waste."

"Okay, so, tell us what you'll be looking for here off Isla de los Perdidos," Henry urged, adjusting the lens. Julie had been really happy with his work in Cameroon last year, and Val began to see why. He had a casual ease about him when holding a camera that hadn't been there the night before when they'd first met. Without that mass of tech, plastic, and glass between them, he was shy and a little twitchy. Now he was calm, prompting her with questions and wording it just-so in hopes of getting the right frame of an answer.

"We're really just going to start off today by chumming the water and throwing out a few chunks of bait to see what we can bring up. Here, off Isla de los Perdidos, we're kind of in No Man's Land. We have some pretty good guesses what we'll find, but the sharks here haven't been studied or tagged. It'll be interesting to see what we've got." Hopefully, they'd get some interest. It wasn't something that could be guaranteed, but everyone loved a good shot of a shark taking a bite out of the surface. "If it looks interesting, we'll drop some cages and get in the water."

Henry smiled behind the camera, nodding. "Great. Okay, tell us about your worst day on the job," he prompted before tensing. His face pulled away from the camera to look back at her, blanching. He scrambled for what to say or how to take it back. Everyone had seen that video of her. The one where she was hit by a twenty-foot great white and carried into the air like a rag doll caught between those jaws. Everyone had seen her being pulled onto the deck of the ship, her body bleeding out and a chunk of her hand missing, skin hanging off her muscles like wet hair. It was replayed every year.

Val smiled to calm him, hand pushing at the air a little between them to assure him that he hadn't offended her. "It's actually not the one you'd think." She leaned back against the table of diving gear. "When I got attacked by that shark, it was over in seconds, and right up until then, it was a beautiful day."

Poppy smiled and went to take another drink of coffee

only to find it empty. She looked around, trying to decide whether or not to take it back to the kitchen before finally putting it down on the other side of the table and walking away, heading for Felix and their gear.

"My sister, Julie, talked me into going with her on a trip to South America once," Val explained for the camera and Henry. "If you've ever seen any of Julie's work before, you know she's an off-road sort of traveler. She likes to discover things no one else has seen before. She likes to be the first to climb a peak or find a species of frog that was thought to be extinct." Val rolled her eyes at this point as though that was particularly dull when, in fact, even she knew it was pretty damn interesting. "Anyway, there I was, in the middle of the rainforest. No water but constant rain. So humid you can barely breathe and so loud. Oh, man, I couldn't believe how loud it was. The animals and plants constantly moving. I'm talking about sounds that you can't even begin to guess at, all night long. And the insects! More insects than grains of dirt."

Val shook her head, glancing past Henry to see her sister walking closer, looking smug as soon as she realized what she was talking about. "Do you know what terrestrial leeches are?" Val asked the camera. "Leeches, the blood-sucking little monsters that wiggle under your clothing and latch their tiny teeth into your flesh, but these ones aren't in some mucky lake or pond. They're on the ground. They stretch themselves up, sensing the nearness of a warm body, and grab onto your boots when you walk past. They climb up your clothing until they find a way in." She emphasized the horror for the camera. "We're talking leeches everywhere. Everywhere." Val shook her head. "No. Give me the deep any day over that nonsense."

Julie laughed and shook her head. Henry reached out

to nudge her forward into the shot, and Julie let him, walking over to stand closer to her sister. "You're really going to pretend that leeches are worse than a shark ripping you apart?"

"Terrestrial leeches," Val said again, raising an eyebrow as though the name itself should answer the question.

Julie huffed out a thin laugh. "I can't even believe you can still get in the water after what happened," she admitted.

"It's amazing," Felix added, coming to toss down two duffel bags close to the stairs.

"Amazing or stupid?" Julie mumbled.

Val shot her a look. "I was bitten once. How many animals have bitten you over the years?"

Julie laughed, and Val could see that she wanted to reply, maybe to point out that none of those bugs and reptiles had ever taken her finger. She wouldn't say it though. Maybe because she worried it would be bad luck. A snake in the jungle could end her life just as easily as a shark in the sea could end Valarie's.

Zach, Julie's fiancé, came down from the wheelhouse. "We should be getting ready to go ashore," he said, sounding almost as eager as Julie did. They really were a match made for the jungle.

Henry shifted anxiously, suddenly rushed. "Okay, Val, tell us a little about Felix's new show coming out next season."

"The one about sharks in South Africa?" Val asked, looking at her ex for the first time. He was already smiling at her. He nodded once, and she turned to the camera again, smiling tightly. "Felix Alvarado is great at his job. If he's getting in the water, you're going to want to see it. He's a thrill seeker turned ocean junkie."

Henry smiled behind his lens and thanked her before turning away and following Zach and Julie as they got their gear together. They stood at the edge of the deck to have the island at their backs when they talked about the plan for arrival. They were going to have to take the speedboat Felix had arrived on out to the edge of the reef and then swim to shore with their supplies in large floaties tethered together. The waves beyond the reef were just too much for any boat to handle.

Val watched them, aware of Felix's attention still on her. She had always been able to feel when he was looking at her, that gaze so intense that it made her skin tight. He sighed in defeat when she wouldn't look back at him, and he moved closer, turning to lean against the table beside her. He smelt the same as always, warm and sweet, the same apple shampoo. His black hair was cut just short enough that he didn't have to fuss with it to keep it in form. It was usually wet anyway. One broad shoulder brushed hers, his hand on the edge of the table so their fingers just barely touched.

"Those were nice things you said." His voice was deep, just the way she remembered it. She hated how much she loved hearing his voice again. "But you say it like you didn't have any part in it. I was fine jumping from planes and climbing mountains before you showed me the ocean."

"You asked to see it. I was a tour guide." She downplayed her role in the beginning. She always did.

He shook his head slowly. "You showed me my life, *mi sol.*" He slipped in one of his favorite nicknames to try to soften her up. He was still watching Julie and Zach talking to the camera, giving her a chance to look at him. She missed him, but that only made her angrier at him. "How long are you going to be mad about Guadalupe?"

Val let out a breath that sounded more like a hiss. "It was stupid, and you should have listened to me."

"I did listen. I just decided not to chicken out." Felix smiled, turning his head to the side to look at her. She looked away. "*Mi sol...*" He pleaded for some sign of mercy.

"It's not about chickening out when people's lives are involved," Val persisted, her voice low but full of anger. Two years hadn't changed that. "It was dangerous. We lost a boat, and two of our crew ended up in the hospital."

Felix pushed off the table to turn and look at her, his square jaw tight and his eyes full of worry. He had hoped she would have cooled down by now. He hadn't really believed her when she said she was leaving after the trip to Guadalupe went south. It hadn't been the first time she'd made that threat when he did something risky. "No one died, Val. Why are you so angry about this one? You never batted an eye at danger when it was just you and me. I've filmed you free-diving with sharks a dozen times."

Val shook her head and stubbornly stared past him, watching the island now. There were clouds above it, gathered around the dark peak, and a haze in the air that meant it was raining over that lush jungle.

"How many times can I explain this to you, Felix?" She dragged her eyes from Isla de los Perdidos to look up at her ex. "It's okay to risk our own lives. It's our passion. But it's not okay to risk the lives of our crew."

He groaned as though she'd struck him. "It's not like I wrecked the boat myself."

She pushed off the table to stand up straight, still not as tall as him, but close. "You knew the weather was bad. You knew we shouldn't have been out that day. I told you."

An awkward silence stretched between them, made

worse when Calvin came down the stairs from the wheel-house. He stopped for half a second, smiled at the obvious lovers' spat, and then tipped his head toward Felix. "Welcome aboard," Calvin greeted before walking past them, clapping the other man on the shoulder.

He spread his arms in exaggerated annoyance when he neared the land team. "Why isn't all of this stuff loaded yet?" Calvin complained loudly, gesturing to the large black bags of supplies.

Val took it as an opportunity to escape and brushed past Felix to help load the little boat. She even went so far as to join Calvin onboard, driving Julie, Zach, Henry, and Megan out to the reef. Henry was dedicated to filming the adventurers while Megan seemed much more focused on getting to land. She was more interested in the wildlife and not nearly as comfortable on boats as the rest of them.

There was some worry about one of the floating bags having been repaired last minute. Julie was sure everything would be fine while Zach was less convinced until the bag bobbed sufficiently in the water, putting all doubts to rest. Julie had an unyieldingly positive outlook on her adventures. Most found it intolerable after weeks of walking and sleeping in the wild, including Valarie, but Zach often called it one of her best qualities.

When all five supply bags and all four adventurers were in the water, Val wished them luck and waved them off. She and Calvin waited on the boat to see them make it to shore. It wasn't a short swim. Their heads and supplies bobbed in the water, disappearing behind swells before reappearing a little farther along.

When they climbed onto the beach, Julie stood up to wave back at them.

Calvin turned the speedboat around and headed back

to the ship. They would check in with the land team to-night via radio and make sure they'd reached their first campsite. Zach liked to keep things orderly and had a general travel plan left behind on the ship so that they could track them if need be. Zach was the "better safe than sorry" kind of explorer, and it was a good thing, too, because Julie would have happily marched off into the unknown without leaving a trail.

Val worried that her sister and Zach would get married in a jungle when they did finally tie the knot. It would be just like Julie to make her trudge out into the land of giant spiders, venomous snakes, and terrestrial leeches just to hear her say "I do."

They got back to the Charlene. Oliver stood on deck, looking pissed; the sun made his orange hair impossibly bright. They barely had time to secure the smaller boat before he started hurling equipment on board.

"Don't you fuckin' move, Cal!" Oliver shouted, tossing the underwater cameraman the plastic trunk with his equipment in it. "I'm not wasting any more time."

Maeko appeared only slightly more awake now than she had stumbling out of her cabin that morning, though she'd managed to get dressed in a wetsuit and haul her rebreather and flippers to the side of the deck. Val started to suspect the other marine biologist of faking exhaustion to avoid interacting with Oliver. It wouldn't surprise her if Maeko perked right up once she was underwater study-ing the reef.

"You going to be able to film both of them at the same time?" Val asked, suddenly worried they'd brought too few cameramen.

"I attached cameras to their suits, so they'll collect some footage themselves. I'll be focusing on the big shots of shipwrecks and the reef," he said, but still sounded skeptical.

Just from the one night she'd spent with Oliver and Maeko, it was clear they both had very different goals for this trip. Maeko had zero interest in salvaging, and Oliver wasn't going to waste time on anything he couldn't bring up and sell.

"Shut up and get ready to go," Oliver barked.

"I haven't even put on my wetsuit!" Calvin complained, putting down the camera trunk.

Val climbed out of the boat and onto the ship.

"Change on the damned boat then!" Oliver threw a wetsuit at Calvin.

Val grabbed the handrails and launched herself up the bridge ladder to the wheelhouse. She opened the door and leaned in against the frame. Chatter between Lochner and his first mate, Ed, stopped abruptly. Ed was still smiling widely at whatever Lochner had been saying, his eyes fixed on the captain, perhaps waiting for a punchline. Lochner, on the other hand, appeared utterly unfazed by the intruder or the shouting on the deck that followed her in. He had one hand on the wheel and the other lifting his mug to his lips, the ones she imagined existed but could barely see beneath his beard.

"Salvage team is getting ready to head out," Val said, earning her Ed's attention and a stiff nod before he shuffled out of the wheelhouse and past her to climb down the ladder. He would be the one driving the divers out to their site by the reef and back. It was a boring task, waiting around for the divers to come back up, but Ed didn't seem to mind.

Val paused a second longer, basking in the curious presence of Kevin Lochner. The beard and his size made him look older than he was. She imagined he wasn't much older than Calvin or herself. Wanting to prolong their interaction out of curiosity, Val added, "We can go farther out from the island and start chumming after they depart." It was a question, even though she hadn't actually put a question in there anywhere.

Lochner nodded. "Julie and the others get to shore?" he asked, knowing they had. Neither Val nor Calvin were new to the job, and they wouldn't have left without making sure they were on the sand.

Val smiled wide because he had given her a stretch of words. It was his way of being friendly, she suspected. "Yes, captain," she said with a smile before backing out of the doorway and letting it close behind her. She turned back toward the deck, looking down at it and the little boat bobbing beside the Charlene. Calvin stood stark naked now, having stripped out of his t-shirt and jeans but keeping on his sunglasses. His body, lean and tan, and flaccid dick was more than enough to wake up Maeko.

"Stop wasting time!" Oliver practically frothed.

"You told me to change on the boat!" Calvin shouted back, always one to match sound levels.

Poppy came up from below deck to see what all the fuss was about just in time to catch Calvin shaking his hips to have his dick helicoptering, his arms spread wide and his smile smug just to make Oliver turn a new shade of red.

Poppy exploded with laughter, and Oliver threw a pair of fins at Calvin.

The cameraman caught them easily, smiling brightly and adding them to the pile of supplies on the boat before setting about the task of pulling his wetsuit up his legs and waist. Oliver was momentarily pacified and hurried about getting their things onboard before turning his temperamental gaze to Maeko. She'd sat down for the show, watching Calvin wiggle into his wetsuit. When Oliver turned tomato red, glaring at her, the marine biologist raised her hands in wordless defeat and got up.

She shot Val one last look before climbing down the ladder. "If Calvin or I don't come back, you know who to have walk the plank."

Val laughed and nodded, rounding the deck. "Good luck," she called before going below to get changed and tell Felix that they would be heading out soon.

She found him in his cabin, the door open. His duffel bag was on the narrow bed, unzipped. He dug around in the pile of clothing and belongings. The clothes were new, different from the last time she saw him, but the bag was the same. He'd been hauling that same green canvas sack with him all over the world. She'd even seen him jump off a rowboat once to get it back from the waves.

When asked, he always gave different answers. He'd convinced Poppy that it was lucky, but more often than not, he just shrugged off its value. Val knew that it belonged to his father. It was the bag he had taken on camping trips when Felix was a boy. He had a memory of one of those trips and his dad using the bag like a pillow at night. It was a random memory, one plucked from a hundred others but made precious simply by being the one that stayed when others faded. His dad died when Felix was still a kid, not even ten years old. When he was a teen, he'd found the duffel bag in the garage and been dragging it around ever since.

Val had stood quietly too long, watching him without him realizing it. She rolled the back of her knuckles against the inside of his doorframe. "Cal and the others are heading out. I'm going to get changed, and then we can get this show rolling." She had planned to sound hard and agitated, but the words came out familiar and comfortable. It was too easy to fall back into routines with him, even now, years later. Being near him was like going home. More than she had ever belonged anywhere in the world, she belonged with him.

His shoulders twisted at the sound of her voice, head turning to look back at her while still digging around in that bag. "Sounds great." He smiled, and she backed away because it made her want to come closer. "Wait, wait!" Felix called, finally pulling something out of his bag. It made crinkling sounds, a crisp plastic wrapper well abused by travel. "Before I forget or eat it myself..." He took a step closer and held out the brightly colored bag. Its contents almost shamed the wrapping, brighter still and coated in sour sugar.

Val smiled skeptically and crossed her arms to keep from reaching out to take the offering. "Bribery?"

Felix's grin didn't falter, his body leaning closer. "A gift, *sirenita*." He used another nickname for her, one he'd started calling her after the first time they dove together. It almost worked. She almost reached out to take those sour sweets from him. They were one of her favorites. So was he.

Val took another step back. It hurt something in her to reject him even in that small way, to leave him holding something out to her like that. But it was so little and so late. "I'm going to get ready. I'll meet you up top." She forced out the words and made herself turn away from him. It never got easier. She didn't look back because she wasn't sure what would hurt her more: to see him still holding out that little offering or to see that he had given up already.

Chapter 4

An hour later, the salvage team had gone, and the Charlene moved away from the island.

Val heaved another bucket of chum into the water behind them, creating a slick in their waves. The water churned red, and she twisted back to signal Poppy to tell Lochner to stop the boat. Felix came up from below deck, his wetsuit up around his waist and his chest bare. Val tried not to look if only to help pretend she wasn't impressed. Sometimes he made lying hard. A tattoo curled over his left shoulder and down his back. She knew it well and didn't have to struggle to remember all its shades of blue, gray, black, and white. A churning depiction of the sea, waves against his shoulder as though they might spill down his front, and against his shoulder blade at his back were the twisting bodies of sharks.

She'd always wondered about his choice when it came to that piece, not because of the ink itself but because of the sharks. A tiger shark was the focal point, and in the dark shadows of its depths moved the distinctive tails of threshers. She had expected a great white when he said he would get a tattoo of their work. Whites were the sharks that came to mind first, after all. They were the ones people wanted to see, the ones they chummed the depths to entice up to the surface.

Felix had two huge chunks of fish with him and slapped them down on the deck. He tied the end of a thick rope around the bait, the other end already laced through the pulleys overhead. The bait was almost the size of her torso.

"Hopeful?" Val asked.

Her ex smiled. "Always, love." He pulled hard at the rope. "See anything yet?" he asked, loud enough for the question to be open to both Val beside him and Poppy in the perch.

"Nothing," Poppy called down.

The cages rattled where they were strung up on either side of the back end of the ship, ready to be dropped today if they saw anything worthwhile.

"Wait," Poppy corrected. As Val looked, the young woman leaned out of her perch and over the back end of the ship. She squinted before she smiled, calling down in a pitch of excitement, "Company!"

Felix joined Valarie at the railing. The morbid slick of blood and guts they'd dumped into the ocean churned, bits of fish fluttering down into the waters. Shadows moved beneath.

"Six. Seven." Poppy counted for them above. "Eight. What are they?"

Val leaned out, palms pushing against the metal railing. They were bulky, thick sharks. Big, but not Kajsa big. Two went after the same chunk in the water, thrashing at the surface. Val smiled. "Bull sharks!"

Felix grabbed a bucket of fish and lifted it up, pinning it between the railing and his thigh. It was all familiar, working with him—still the same routine even after two years apart. She reached into the bucket with both hands, pulled out a fish and tossed it into the water. No sooner had it smacked down on the surface when teeth came up to snatch it.

"Ten. Eleven. Twelve," Poppy continued to count.

"Looks like we have silkies, too," Val said.

Felix nodded and pointed at another, larger shark coming up to the surface to join the feeding frenzy. "Tiger." He took a fish and threw it out.

Val laughed in excitement. "Looks like this is a pretty good spot after all." She left his side to grab the camera. She'd already prepared the settings and taken some practice shots before they started chumming. She flipped out the viewing screen in front of her face and turned it on. The camera came to life, and she leaned her hip into the corner of the rear railing of the ship for an anchor. The day was beautiful, the colors vivid, and Felix looked great. He hurled out fish, and the frenzy of sharks swirled to take the easy meal.

Felix narrated, telling the camera about the different sharks and how this area is particularly secluded. "Due to mysticism and folklore, the mainland locals won't come out this far toward the island of Los Perdidos, not even to fish. They say there are monsters in these depths and that the waters themselves are angry." He smiled wide at the possibilities, finding excitement where others found fear. "Whether they have good reason or not, it means the fishing around the island is pretty much nonexistent. And if there's a good population of fish around the island reef, that means we have a good chance of seeing some big predators." He leaned out and pointed off the back of the ship, and she turned the camera to follow.

Tails cut the surface, and bull sharks grappled for the chunks of chum in the water. They bumped one another hard, bodies twisting and thudding against the boat. Felix was so busy looking, he almost forgot to narrate. "These have to be some of the biggest bull sharks we've ever seen, possibly the largest recorded." New excitement edged into his voice. "We'll have to film them along the ship to get measurements."

A tiger shark, easily more than fifteen feet, came up when he leaned out, forcing the other toothy fish to move out of its way. It broke the surface with hungry jaws agape just below Felix. For half a second Val held her breath, fingers turning white where they clenched the camera.

That slick body wriggled, mouth open and teeth bared just under his outstretched arm. His eyes went wide, but his smile only grew when he looked right down into that throat. It snapped angrily when it couldn't reach high enough and sunk back down into the depths.

Val let out a breath. "Shit," she muttered.

Felix laughed the way he always did when a little shaken and stepping back from the edge. Val moved closer, filming the fish in the water, watching them bump the camera she'd already dropped in and attached to the back for underwater footage. If they didn't knock it loose, she might end up with some great shots of the frenzy.

The silky sharks grappled with the bull sharks, shoving for space, snapping jaws at the slop on the surface. And then, all at once, they left. She watched through the viewfinder as they slipped away, all of them, back into the depths.

"Felix," she exhaled, looking over the camera to see the water herself. Something else was rising up from the depths.

"White!" Poppy shouted from her perch just before Val

saw the shadow rising off to the side, circling the back of the boat. It was a big shadow.

Felix pulled the rope, and the rigging squealed, lifting the chunk of fish high and swinging it out. The hunk of tuna slapped against the water, and he let it sink a little before yanking it up again. Just as he started to pull, that great shadow rushed in. Val held the camera steady and bit back a curse when the giant came in to roll along the side of the boat, following the bait Felix pulled. Lips peeled back, and gums receded; rows of jagged, white teeth cut at the water, wishing to cut at so much more. That head broke the surface to follow the chunk of fish; one eye rolled back, and jaws snapped wildly but not quite catching the offering.

It lingered there, alongside the boat.

"Are you getting this?" Felix shouted in excitement.

"She has to be at least twenty-five feet!" Poppy called down, using the side of the boat and experience to measure.

Val smiled. A new record. "He," she said when the great beast of a fish sunk back into the water, turning and circling the back end of the boat, looking for another chance. "That's a he," she said, voice quieter than she'd like to admit. He was a monster of a fish, but females were usually bigger.

"Poppy, get down here!" Felix called, voice ringing with excitement.

Poppy slid down from her perch and landed in a squat before shooting upright again. She ran to his side and took the rope from his hands. The bait flew out again, hitting the water before she started yanking hard. The chunk of tuna burst up from the ocean, and the shark followed, breaking the surface and rising higher. More than half its body came up before it crashed down.

"You better be ready to let that go if he gets it," Val said, hands steady to get the shots. She was so busy filming that she didn't even notice Felix suiting up and pulling at the ropes to drop the shark cages into the water.

She didn't take notice until he stood behind her, putting her air tank on her back and buckling it around her waist. Val craned her neck to look back at him, already lacing one arm through the strap. "You really want to go in there?" she asked, even though she knew the answer. A smile spread her lips. She changed hands on the camera to lace the other through the shoulder strap. He pulled at the tabs to tighten them.

"What should we name him?" Felix asked rather than answering her question. He pulled on his own tanks, buckling up and moving their flippers and masks closer to the edge.

He got up and straddled the railing along the back of the boat, one foot on each side and hands held out to help her over. She wanted to call him crazy, but he was, and always had been, her kind of crazy.

She turned off her camera, missing another beautiful breach as Poppy continued to play with their new shark. Val put the camera into one of the padded tubs and picked up the other she'd taken out, the one with a handle on either side and a giant lens for underwater shots.

"George," she decided, hurrying back to Felix. She pulled on her flippers while he put on her mask. He hoisted her up to the ledge by her forearms while she held the camera. She swung her legs over, the blue ocean slapping against the white of the boat and rocking the cages just below the surface.

Felix's fingers tightened on her arm when George swam by. They both watched him with the sensation that he was looking back at them, his tail flicking to make those cages thump against the back of the boat.

"Ready?" Felix asked.

She stood on that ledge and put the mouthpiece of her oxygen tank between her lips. She watched the opening at the top of her cage while Felix watched the shark. She held her camera close to her belly with both hands.

"Go," he said, and she jumped.

The world went quiet. Not silent, but quiet. She sank down into the bottom of her cage and stayed there, turning on her camera and testing out the settings on the great open sea around her. When a shadow cut over her, she twisted up to film George from beneath as he circled the boat again. She stood, getting her bearings, and pushed the camera and her arms out the viewing hole to film the shark as he moved deeper, leaving the hunk of fish for a moment to circle her instead.

The cage shuddered, bobbed, and then started to move. Either Felix or Poppy was turning the crank to shift her away from the boat. The chains rattled, making strange sounds in the water, the surface rippling around the top four edges. George seemed more interested when she moved, coming in closer, baring teeth for the camera and nudging the cage.

He swam between her and the boat, and in the background of the shot, she saw Felix drop down into the second cage. George whipped around to investigate, and she filmed the massive fish closing in on Felix's cage to take a closer look. The body of the shark blocked her view of the other cage completely, and then, seemingly from out of nowhere, a second shark burst up from the deep. Val knocked her shoulder against the bars but held fast to her camera. The second, larger shark shot straight up under George, caught his belly in her jaws and continued to thrust upward.

They breached the surface together, but with their combined weight, the flight was short-lived. They crashed back down and onto Felix's cage. The whole back of the ship dipped down, pulled violently until either the cables or the rigging snapped. The sharks thrashed, stirring air into the water turned red with blood.

Val continued to hold the camera on reflex but stopped thinking about the shot. She stared over it in disbelief at the scene. The new shark, even larger than George, thrashed against the back of the boat atop the shark cage. She couldn't see Felix through the writhing bodies of beasts and churning waters. Her heart sank low in her stomach when Felix's cage dropped out from behind the fighting giants. She leaned hard into the front of her cage to see him slipping down into the dark, but the cage was empty. A sliver of relief washed over her, her body leaning forward into the bars and exhaling a gust of bubbles. Her gaze tore up to the fight again, suddenly horrified that he might be in those waters with the monster sharks.

Before she could worry about whether or not he had gotten out of the sea and into the boat, her own cage bobbed. Had the rigging really given way? Was her cage cut loose? It bobbed again, sinking lower, more than a meter from the surface now. Biting at her breather, she let go of the camera with one hand and pushed herself upward. Grabbing onto one edge of her cage and pulling, Val launched herself high enough to have her head break the surface. Water clung to her goggles and daylight gleamed, making her squint.

Felix stood on deck, and even from this distance she could tell he was shouting, arms pulling with all his weight to try to turn the crank and drag her cage back in. It must have been stuck. They couldn't reel her back to the boat. Lochner had left the wheelhouse, shouting something back to Felix and then pointing up at the rigging. Val looked up, squinting against the sun. The rigging had bent, half attached now where bolts ripped out and only struggling cables kept it together. Those cables were the ones still attached to her cage—dragging her in closer to the ship and closer to the sharks thrashing about the waters between.

Felix twisted to the side to look back at her. She was going to collide with the great whites. There was a chance she could survive just bunkered down in her vessel. There was a chance they would stop any second now and vanish into the deep. The water churned red, spraying into the air when a tail cut across the surface. There was also a chance they would push her cage down enough to snap those cables, or whatever fastened them to the ship, and she would have no choice but to swim up through that bloody water or sink to the bottom and eventually drown.

It seemed that the very moment she made her choice to abandon the cage, Felix climbed over the railing along the side of the ship and dove into the waters off the port. She pulled her legs up out of the cage and pushed off the metal railing. It was hard to swim away from the boat, away from safety rather than toward it, but she had to get distance from the struggle in the water. She sunk down below the surface just enough to escape the splashing on the surface, breather exhaling bubbles and fins propelling her forward. She cut an arch in the blue, inelegant in the company of creatures made to swim.

The sharks had stopped their wild brawl. George bobbed at the surface, missing large chunks of flesh. Bits of him floated in the waters all around. The champion opened her mouth to slide back a piece of George, circling him comfortably. Valarie kept kicking, kept swimming, moving closer to the side of the boat. Felix grabbed her as soon as he reached her, pulling her by the arm to propel her forward faster. They both hugged the side of the Charlene when they surfaced. Felix reached up, and Lochner was there, grabbing his arm to lift him until he could get a hold of the railing himself.

Val looked back down into the water around her. The silky sharks had returned, one pushing her up against the boat as it rushed past. The great white champion must have moved away if the others were coming in for their mouthfuls.

Felix, still hanging on the side of the boat, pulled Val up out of the water by her wrist.

"Grab her!" he shouted, and Lochner grabbed her other arm and pulled until he was able to hook an arm around her middle and lift her over the railing, dumping her onto the deck. Val spat out her mouthpiece and struggled out of her pack before collapsing. She lay there for a moment, panting for air and looking up at the blue sky. The dangling rigging creaked, the cable rattling against the gears.

Felix fell onto the deck with Lochner's help and hovered over her; she felt his hands running along her arms and legs and torso, searching for any tears in suit or flesh. Finally, he choked out a laugh and took the camera that was still clutched to her chest from her. "And you say I'm reckless." He waved the camera at her.

"You are." Val looked up at him, breath still labored, and cracked a slow smile. "What should we name her?"

He heaved out a laugh just before the rigging gave an awful groan and tore from its bolts. It slapped against the water and sank with the cages. Val looked up, rolling her head against the deck to see Poppy standing there, filming everything. Later, she would watch the footage and see the cage swing through the water to have its cables tangled with dead George and soon dog-piled by sharks looking for a free meal.

She would not regret jumping out beforehand and making a swim for the boat.

Chapter 5

When the sun went down, they gathered around the communal table in the tight dining area.

Poppy started in on a retelling of the day's events aboard the Charlene, explaining to the camera in great detail how they broke the ship. Calvin had been particularly keen to hear just how they managed the damage and, more importantly, who would be paying for repairs. Poppy pushed her laptop in front of him, crowding his plate, and turned on the footage from their shark encounter. For at least a little while, Calvin completely forgot about repairs.

Maeko came around and sat on the other end, making Poppy, Felix, and Val scoot down. Poppy nearly sat on top of Ed to be closer to Calvin and the laptop. She had watched the footage maybe a hundred times already and still whistled and gasped like the first.

Maeko, on the other hand, had seen it once and that was enough. She stabbed her spaghetti and twirled the pasta around her fork, the sleeve of her thick sweater falling down her arm. The cuff almost caught a glob of tomato sauce before she shoved it back up to her elbow. "You should come take a look at the reef tomorrow," she said, turning toward Val. "I found species there that don't even belong in these parts and most are bigger than I've ever seen before." She ended her sentence by stuffing a forkful of pasta into her mouth.

Val took a drink of her water from the old, blue plastic cup. One side had been mangled by someone gnawing at it, teeth bending and pulling at the plastic until it became rough threads. It reminded her of something from her child-hood, though without the teeth marks. Just about every-thing in the kitchen cabinets and drawers reminded her of her grandmother's house. It occurred to her, grimly, that some of these things could have been her grandmother's. She had passed away long ago, and Val had no idea where her cups and plates and violent-looking grapefruit spoons had gone.

If she found one of those grapefruit weapons in the pile of spoons, she'd ask Lochner about where all this junk came from. Until then, she drank her water and nodded at Maeko. "Might as well. Without the cages, we can't do more than draw them to the boat and get frenzy shots and bait bites."

Felix took his gaze from the laptop screen to look at the two women to his right. "Because that's suddenly boring? The channel loves that shit, and you can still film with the underwater camera rig. We'll just dangle it off the side." He smiled wide and rolled his fork in his spaghetti. "You just want to get back into the water."

Calvin whistled and closed the laptop at the end of the clip. "And I thought the ones we saw at the reef were big." He took a drink of his beer and shook his head. "You should definitely get more shots of that one. She might be a new record. If we could get her alongside the boat, we could measure her."

"We?" Maeko looked up from her meal, raising a thin eyebrow. "Are you trying to trade teams now?"

Felix smiled but didn't say anything.

Calvin raised his hands. "It's not like we're working against each other."

"No." Maeko shook her head and then looked back over her shoulder toward the closed cabin doors. She leaned against the table and toward Calvin on the other side. "You're not leaving me alone with him. You heard him to-day. He wanted to destroy a portion of the reef!" she whis-per-yelled.

Val looked up at that. "What?"

Calvin sighed. "Part of the reef has grown off of old sunken ships."

"It's amazing!" Maeko added, grabbing Val's arm and turning toward her. "We're talking old, old ships. Like from the 1600s. It's become the skeleton of the reef."

"And Oliver, being a salvager, wants to get a better look at those ships."

"Bullshit!" Maeko snapped hotly before looking to the others at the table as though they had become a council, and she set herself to pleading her case. "It took me an hour to convince him to leave it alone and focus on the other ships."

"So, there are others?" Felix prompted.

Maeko snorted. "Others? Dozens. All sorts of ships." She sounded instantly bored, shrugging a shoulder and going back to her spaghetti.

"Small fishing boats, a few yachts, and the skeleton of some much older looking wrecks," Calvin elaborated. "Oliver took some photos and samples to determine which ships they are but wants to go back tomorrow and take a better look inside. I could use the extra cameras if you guys want to come with us." He took another drink, finishing the beer he'd opened when they started making dinner twenty minutes ago. "Maeko keeps taking off to look at the reef, and I can't exactly follow them both."

Val glanced at Felix. "We could do shark bite shots later. We are here for a week."

Felix shrugged. "Shipwrecks could be fun."

"We saw hammerheads," Calvin added to sweeten the deal, and Felix perked up. It wasn't often he got to take a look at hammerhead sharks. The channels usually wanted him filming with great whites or bulls or tiger sharks—the ones that gave people nightmares. Hammerheads had a tendency to stay off the radar when it came to people. Oh, they were there, and everyone knew what one looked like, but they stuck to the coastal bottoms, hunting boney fish and stingrays.

There was something exciting about that, a shark with no interest in chum.

It didn't take much more to convince Felix to help out with the wreckage filming.

"We only just started looking at the ships today. We haven't been inside any, but I know Oliver has plans. He's going to research tonight and decide which ones are most valuable." Calvin rolled his eyes before continuing. "There's at least seven newer ships we spotted—all made and lost in the last fifty years by the looks of them. Oliver got most of the ship names. He got real excited about a submarine stuck right on the edge of the drop-off." He leaned toward Felix, eyes expressing a wealth of frustration. "It took at least ten minutes to convince him not to try to get inside it, and I'm pretty sure he only agreed to leave it alone for today."

Felix smiled. "Sunken sub would make for good TV."

Calvin took another swig of his beer and shook his head. "I'm not interested in popping open a military vessel, and I'm even less interested in playing with a ship that's halfway off the cliff edge. One bubble escapes that thing, and the whole ship might slip right off into the deep."

"Well, it sounds like we've got enough wrecks for a handful of TV specials, even without it." Felix agreed.

Calvin nodded. "Now just convince that nutbag of that tomorrow, and we'll have a smooth dive."

Julie had been right. This place was a treasure trove of sights. Even if she didn't find anything of interest on her island, there would be more than enough from the ocean teams to make the voyage worthwhile to her backers.

Thinking of her sister, Val looked at the beat-up, motion-powered, waterproof masterpiece on her wrist. She'd had the same watch for nearly five years, and it never failed her.

"Shit." She shoveled a last bite of spaghetti into her mouth and then scooted into Maeko. "Gotta go," she said with her mouth full. Felix laughed at her, but she didn't look back at him. Maeko rolled out just long enough to let her pass before sitting back down.

Val chewed and swallowed on her way to her cabin, pushing the thin panel of wood open and letting it swing shut behind her. The bed took up exactly half of the tiny room, narrow and wedged in between walls. Her green sleeping bag was a rumpled mess on top of the thin mattress with a pillow somewhere underneath. The swing of the door had taken one-quarter of the space, and in that last quarter of unoccupied room was a narrow ledge for a desk. Her laptop sat there, plugged in so she only had to tap it to life.

Val sat on the edge of her bed and watched the screen come to life. It took a few minutes for the tracking program to log in and catch up, but soon enough there was a rough map of the island, green as seen from above, and a red arrow where Julie's emergency tracker had last sent its signal.

Val picked up her walkie-talkie and turned the knob. A soft static was interrupted when she thumbed down the button, already smiling even before she started talking. She did a formal, deep voice. "Land team. Come in, land team. This is the SS Charlene. Come in, land team." She let go of the button and waited, light static filling the room.

Julie had taken a walkie-talkie for emergency communication reasons, in case she needed to contact the wheelhouse, but Val had set the secondary walkie-talkie to the same channel so they could keep in touch. She held the button down again. "Julie, get off your fiancé and answer the call," she said in her normal voice this time, letting go of the button and waiting another few seconds before pushing it down again impatiently. "Julie DeNola, you answer that walkie right now. Don't make me come over to that island."

She let go of the button and waited. The static fizzed on the line. She had always felt that static was worse than silence. It was sound between sounds, leaving the ear thinking it heard things and always on edge to catch the reply. Val sighed and looked at the ping on the map. It was right where Zach said they would make camp on the first night, so at least they were on course.

The static grew louder, and she looked at the black plastic speaker. For a moment, it seemed to be gushing sounds. Static, yes, but something more beneath it. A humming, groaning, throaty sound. Val lifted it higher, holding it closer to her ear. A voice gurgled beneath the static, she was sure of it, but it didn't say anything. It made sounds, guttural and deep.

"Valarie!" Julie shouted over the speaker, replacing the strange static.

Val jumped where she sat, clutching the walkie-talkie hard and letting out a breathy laugh.

She smiled and pushed down the button. "Here. Can you hear me?"

There was a pause of static and then that familiar voice again. "I hear you. I think we're getting some kind of inter-ference." Her voice crackled near the end.

Val nodded even though her sister couldn't see it. "Okay. How's the island?" She cut to the point.

Another pause and Val thought maybe she'd lost her. "It's incredible," Julie reported at last. "We found the old prison. Creepy as shit." She laughed. "And this place, it's just, so different."

Val remembered her talking about the prison. One of the failed attempts at putting this island to use more than a hundred years ago. "What do you mean by different?" she asked when static returned between them.

There was a delay, but this time she knew Julie would answer.

"I think we have enough footage for a whole season and we've only been here a day," she said, and Val frowned, not sure how that was an answer. "There are plants here I've never seen before, and some of these animals shouldn't even be in this part of the world. And some of them... You should have seen the crocodiles, Val!" Julie gushed, voice crackling in and out at times.

Val thought back to the giant sharks they'd seen that

day and wondered just how much bigger a crocodile could get. She supposed it was endless, if nothing in the environment stopped them.

"And there was a jaguar and—" Her voice garbled with background sounds. A mess of voices close by. Someone shouting.

Val looked at the speaker like it might have a screen. "Is that Megan? What's going on?" She sounded upset. Really upset.

The walkie-talkie crackled for another second before Julie answered. "Yeah, she's got a bit of jungle fever." She laughed a little, the sound of it clipped and uncomfortable. "I think she'll calm down after she gets some sleep. How are things on your end? Have you seen any sharks? Did Oliver find any wrecks?" Julie asked, sounding hopeful again. Val could hear other voices chattering in the background now.

"Oliver found a bunch of wrecks and is very excited." Val did not sound at all excited for him. "And we did see some sharks. They broke the boat," she added for the sake of drama.

"They what? You broke the boat?"

"How could I break the boat? It was the sharks," Val countered.

"You—the sharks are—I shouldn't have—alone." Julie cut in and out more now, but Val got the bulk of the lecture.

She laughed and held down the button. "You're breaking up. Everything is fine. We're doing great. We'll see you in four days." She let go of the button.

"—days. Love—" Came Julie's choppy voice.

Val smiled. "Love you, too," she said before lying back on her bed. She let the walkie-talkie sit there, fizzing with static for a while before finally turning it off. If Julie had trouble out there, she could contact the ship directly, and if things got really bad, she had an emergency beacon to call in a rescue team. Val had never loved the idea of her sister in some dark forest at night, surrounded by wild creatures with little more than a nylon tent for protection. She wondered if Julie had similar feelings about her spending so much time on the ocean.

She rolled onto her side and reached under the bed to drag out a duffel bag. It was already open and only took her a couple seconds to fish out some clean underwear, a long night shirt, and her towel. She put them down on the bed and stood up. She pulled off her shirt and wiggled out of her jeans, kicking them off when they were low enough and leaving them where they landed on the floor. She lifted her black and gray sports bra over her head. She was just about to take off her underwear when she caught her own reflection in the mirror fixed to the back of the door.

Val turned to one side, the side without scars, the one with smooth, deeply tanned skin and tight muscles. And then she turned the other way. Her skin puckered around those old scars, spread out over her torso, arm, thigh, and back in a way that looked utterly random. If she hadn't been bent the way she had, if she hadn't been caught in those teeth so awkwardly, she might have lost something she couldn't live without. Her arm stretched out toward her reflection, three fingers touching the glass to meet with their image and that scar tissue where her pinkie had been gleaming bright and pale. Val smiled at her reflection and dropped her hand away from the mirror. She pushed down her underwear and wrapped that thick purple towel around herself before scooping up her pajamas from the bed. On her way out, she grabbed the little plastic baggie of toiletries from beside the door.

In the mouth of the narrow hall, she glanced toward the previously filled common area. Only Calvin and Lochner sat there now. A couple more beers crowded the table and Calvin gestured with his arms, describing something from his day's adventures to his husband while Lochner ate dinner and, every so often, nodded. She turned away and was almost to the bathroom when she heard a sound she'd never heard before. She looked back. She couldn't see the table anymore, but she could hear Lochner laughing. Val smiled to herself and pulled the pocket door into an open slide, taking one step into the bathroom before realizing that it was occupied.

The shower was on. Warm steam greeted her, rolling out around her ankles.

She stood there, just inside the bathroom, holding onto the door and watching the man in the corner of the shower, beneath the spray of hot water. His back was to her, stark naked and dripping wet. His arms came up to meet his face beneath the shower spray, pushing his dark hair up and back. She watched all those muscles move and, despite herself, found it difficult to swallow. She closed the door behind her and Felix turned to peel his face from the water and open his eyes. He grinned wide. He didn't rush to turn around, moving slow. His smile only grew when he took her in, noting her towel. "I can share," Felix offered, hands running down his front to sweep water from his chest and abdomen.

Val would have liked to have been able to say that she'd at least hesitated, but she hadn't. She put her clean clothes on top of his on the edge of the sink and hung up her towel. She loved the way he watched her, as though he hadn't seen her naked a thousand times before. She took the tie from her hair to let it fall loose, then pulled the body wash from her toiletries bag. He reached out toward her to take it. Another routine so easily taken up again. Holding the bottle, he stepped back just enough to let her slip between him and the wall. Val's eyes closed under the water, and her fingers came up to push her hair back, ignoring the electric feeling in her skin with his naked body so close behind hers.

She let the heat of the water soak into her muscles, begging to soothe, but her body was suddenly too aware of his to relax. Two years. She'd left him two years ago, and other than the occasional awkward video chat, she had not seen him since. His hand folded into the side of her waist to move her, gently pushing until she followed, stepping to the side and out of the spray.

She watched him rub his hands together, lathering the soap. She noticed his ring, the pale white gold one that matched hers. Only she didn't wear hers. She kept it on a chain in a tin in her bag, where she could take it out and look at it but never admit she still had it.

"Why are you still wearing that?" Val asked, voice deep and already a little sedate. His hands touched her shoulders, rubbing them with soap that he dragged down her arms.

The air filled with that clean aloe vera and apple scent. He pushed and pulled gently to turn her around, his hands working over her back. She swallowed down a moan and leaned forward, bracing her arms against the cool plastic wall of the shower.

"Because I'm married," he whispered near her ear, his hands rubbing down her hips and over her thighs.

"Divorced. We're divorced."

His face nuzzled into the back of her wet hair, and his mouth found her neck. His body pushed up against the back of hers, and she felt all of him, the spray of the shower bouncing off his side to wash soap suds down her legs. "You say that to people," he mumbled against her skin, his hand sliding over her stomach and then down, cupping between her legs to find more heat than the shower was providing. "But you never filed any papers."

Val hummed. "I forgot," she lied. She'd never wanted to divorce him. She'd never even wanted to leave him, but it had been a matter of principle—and maybe just a little too much pride. She couldn't stay and work with him if he wouldn't change how he did things. So, she left.

"Liar," he whispered before his mouth found her ear.

Her fingers curled against the wall, and her mouth dropped open a little when his fingers moved lower. "Go anywhere," Felix whispered against her ear, rubbing his hips against her ass to grind his erection between her cheeks. "Do anything, Val." He moaned against her neck. "I'll still be yours." Her body shuddered hard between his and the wall.

He leaned back from her long enough to turn her around. She looked up at him through her lashes, his eyes hazy. She pressed her shoulders back against the cold wall. His fingers trailed down her front, and longing parted his lips and pushed a breath up from his chest.

"Say I'm yours," he begged, suddenly tired and desperate. "Val." His fingers came back up, stroking the side of her neck. "Say I'm yours."

She realized then that it was pain she saw in his eyes. She had left him. He had been so cocky about it at the time that she'd convinced herself he didn't care if she came or went. He loved her, she knew that. She'd always known that. But until that moment she hadn't realized that she'd been punishing him when she left.

She swallowed, too much saliva in her mouth. "You're mine," she admitted. "You're always mine."

He let out a breath that shuddered his frame and dropped his head down. His mouth pressed against hers. She'd almost forgotten how plush his lips were and the way he sucked at her bottom lip before ending a kiss. He held her hips and slid down her body until he knelt in the shower.

Her head rolled back against the wall when he lifted her thighs to drape them over his shoulders. Her hands slid into his hair, and soon she couldn't swallow back her sounds.

Chapter 6

The sky hid behind a seemingly endless canopy of gray clouds that had rolled in overnight. A shadow stretched over the island, with thick walls of rain hiding the peak of the mountain.

The island looked darker the closer they came, shadows growing thicker when they bounced off the waters over the reef. Below the surface, things calmed for a moment. Val went with Maeko to film her exploration of the reef while Poppy and Felix followed Calvin and Oliver to the wreckage.

They planned to spend every daylight hour they had gathering footage, but after only an hour, Maeko and Val resurfaced. Ed, waiting for them in the speedboat with a book in hand, jumped in surprise when they broke the surface. They weren't expected back so soon. Maeko spat out her mouthpiece and gasped for air, reaching wildly for the boat. Val grabbed her arm to lift it higher, pushing her up toward Ed so that he could help pull her up into the boat. When he came back to the edge, Val handed him her camera and then climbed the short ladder up and over. She landed with a thump on the floor of the narrow speedboat.

"We were attacked!" Maeko wailed.

Val took out her mouthpiece and then sucked down a few large breaths of clean air.

Ed stared wide-eyed at the two marine biologists, not seeing any obvious wounds. They'd brought up a layer of water that slosh about the boat, but none of it had turned pink or red with blood.

Val raised an apologetic hand to wave off the worried man. "The fish were a little aggressive," she explained.

"A little?" Maeko shouted. "It bit your camera!" She turned to look up at Ed. "One tried to kill me!"

He looked to Val for some sort of denial, but she just shrugged. "It didn't kill her," she concluded. "We're fine. The shots were good."

"Good?" Maeko was still shouting. "They kept coming at us! Pushing! One bit my rebreather!" She twisted, trying to show Ed. He helped her unstrap and remove it.

"It wasn't a good day for a dive," Val confirmed, beginning to remove her own gear. She started with the goggles and flippers and then unbuckled her rebreather. She set them all neatly together in case she decided to go back in, while Maeko kicked everything away from herself like a child refusing to get dressed.

Ed walked back to his seat at the wheel and opened a cooler on the floor. He took out a couple of waters and passed them down. Just as she reached for the bottle he offered, Val noticed his book. The thick paperback had wears on the spine from being held open or maybe even bent back. On the bright lavender cover stood a woman in a ball gown of nearly the same color. Her dangerously low shoulder strap exposed the side of her round breast while a shirtless and very muscular man clung to her, his face lodged in the curve of her neck like his life depended on it. Val couldn't make out the title from where she sat, but the font was curly.

"Interesting." She grinned.

Ed looked at his book and then pressed his lips tight before picking it up. "What?" he asked, sitting down and opening it to start reading again.

"Nothing. Just interesting."

He frowned a little and blushed just slightly. "Everyone likes romance," Ed insisted.

Val nodded and twisted the cap off her water. "Sure. Sure. You read it for the romance."

Ed shot her a pointed look before his expression softened at the still-distressed Maeko. "You all right?" he asked, cringing a little when he suspected the answer.

Anger escaped Maeko in a shrill warcry. "No! I'm not all right! Things tried to eat me, and I want to go back to the ship."

Val took a drink of water and pulled herself to her feet. She crossed the narrow boat to offer Maeko the second bottle. It had gotten rough down there. She tried to downplay it in hopes that Maeko would get over it. They had spent a nice twenty minutes just exploring the reef. Maeko had been delighted with the different creatures and pointing them out to make sure Val got good shots of all of them with the camera. They came across a cluster of nurse sharks tucked up against one wall of the reef, bunkered down together to wait out the day. They were massive, and the sight was daunting even if they weren't man-eaters. Val had let Maeko drift farther along the reef while she lingered to film the resting giants. They weren't really social as far as studies had shown, but they clustered together during the day for safety and waited until night to stalk the reefs and beaches.

Not long after she caught up with Maeko again, they saw the first lemon shark. She filmed it hunting along the reef, eating anything it could get its mouth on. And then the ocean exploded with life. It wasn't just a lemon shark. Handfuls of Caribbean reef sharks appeared, all at least ten feet long. Everything went fine for all of two minutes before the toothy fish took notice of the gangly intruders. The reef sharks were first to get aggressive. Moving in closer and closer. Barreling straight for them only to veer off at the last second. Val had to push more than half a dozen away by the nose just to pull Maeko with her to the surface. She'd lost a chunk out of her flipper but decided not to point it out to the already-frazzled diver.

"It was a great dive up until the sharks," Val tried to console her. Admittedly, Val had a larger tolerance for bad behavior from sharks. As far as she was concerned, if they didn't sink teeth into her skin, it was a good dive.

Maeko took the water bottle angrily, and Val tried not to smile. For some reason, she was being blamed for the behavior of the sharks. She decided not to argue, imagining that it wouldn't make Maeko feel any better. She was shaken. It happened. Maeko didn't dive for the thrill or to push boundaries. She only went underwater because that happened to be where the reefs and marine life she studied were located. She hadn't been overly interested in sharks even before they started pushing her around. She seemed much more interested in the various species of coral and anemones and all of the life living between them.

The plastic bottle crinkled in Maeko's hand when she drank half of it and then took a deep breath of air. "I'm never going down there again," she said, dark eyes a little glassy.

Val laughed and sat down on the bench beside the

woman. "Yes, you are. You're going to go back to the ship, take a shower, and get something to eat, and then you're going to look at the footage from this dive and start writing down notes about what you saw and get all excited about going down again."

Maeko shook her head. "No. No," she mumbled, taking another drink of her water, like maybe this time it would be vodka. "Maybe with a cage or something."

Ed snorted. "Tough time finding a cage thanks to this one." He jabbed a thumb in Val's direction.

She shot him a glare. "That wasn't my fault."

"No. It was a shark. A shark wrecked the cages." Maeko pitched in panic again, dragging in short breaths.

Val put a hand on her shoulder, pressing firmly. "That was in the deep, away from the island, and it was more than one shark." She sighed, shaking that shoulder a little to get Maeko to look back at her. "You're okay. You know more about those fish than most divers. You know that they're predators and they get pushy sometimes. You just push back as much as you need to and then get out of the way. Just like we did."

Maeko nodded once before looking back down at the bottle of water in her hands and then finishing it. It still wasn't vodka.

They spent another forty minutes bobbing in the water just off the reef. Ed read his book, and Maeko reviewed the footage of the coral to calm herself. Val stared off across that short stretch of ocean to the shadowed beaches of the island beneath that seemingly unyielding raincloud. She couldn't imagine Julie having a better day than her in that weather.

The sky rumbled as the clouds from the island spread outward. It looked more like they were growing than moving. Rain pattered loudly across the beach and over the ocean, stretching toward the reef. The surface of the water rippled, wind washing the sound toward them.

"You won't be reading much longer if this keeps up," Val mumbled to Ed.

He huffed in agreement, and she suspected he started reading faster because he didn't bother to look up. Must be at a really romantic part.

They heard the surface breaking when the other dive group came up a half a dozen meters away. Maeko, having collected herself enough by then, helped pull their cameras and gear on board. Poppy bobbed in the water, already telling the elaborate story of their adventure into a sunken ship. She didn't even pause when they were helping her up into the boat. She continued to call what they saw "the kraken," but Felix was quick to insert "giant octopus" every time she did.

Oliver cut in, irate as usual. "Don't we have a spear gun or a bang stick or something back on the ship?" He pulled off his flippers with a huff.

Felix smiled, sideways and full of mischief. "For emergencies, sure..."

"Good. We'll get some of those and come back tomorrow."

Poppy finally went quiet, eyes large. "You can't mean to—"

"I want that beast off my ship!" Oliver raged.

Val helped Felix take off his gear, pressing back a laugh. "I don't know. Sounds like that boat belongs to the octopus, not you, Oliver..."

He shot her a glare and continued to plot a forceful aquatic eviction all the way back to the Charlene.

They barely beat the rain to the larger boat, the storm

seeming to follow them out with rising winds. It only got worse by late afternoon. The ship rocked violently. The rain came and went, returning every so often to wet the decks. The waves churned, bouncing the boat and splashing over the railings.

A couple of hours of rocking and almost everyone got seasick. Poppy, despite being green in the face, still tried to review footage from the morning's dive. A valiant but slow-going effort.

Val handed her another glass of water, holding on to the table with the other hand to keep herself upright. Everything tipped at a sharp angle now, which wouldn't have been so bad if that angle would just stop changing. Poppy took a gulp and then pressed her eyes shut, trying to keep the water down. Val braced herself, watching the younger woman and waiting to see if she'd hurl again. She couldn't have anything left in her but for that one drink of water.

Val touched her head soothingly and smiled. "Give it up, Pop," she pleaded. "Just go lay down until the storm's over."

Poppy opened her eyes and mouth at the same time, taking slow but deep breaths. "I'm good. I'm good."

Val smiled and shook her head. Poppy had always been like this, not even illness could stop her. It could slow her down, sure, but it couldn't stop her. Val had seen Poppy snorkel with a full-blown cold, film with the flu, and even try to dive with a fever. Of course, on that last occasion, her fever had gotten so bad she was hallucinating, and they mostly just let her think she was diving while actually being snuggled up with an air tank.

Calvin swung his head into the room, the door bouncing off the wall and almost slapping him in the face. It would have if he hadn't pushed it back with a knowing hand. The Charlene was his home, and he was more than used to the oddities of living at sea. "Loch wants you up top!" he shouted before disappearing again.

Val assumed he meant her and gave Poppy's shoulder one last squeeze before launching herself toward the door. Somehow getting to the stairs became an uphill battle, while going up them was almost like falling. She hadn't even bothered to grab a jacket, the spray from the waves making her skin damp but not managing to soak through her sweatshirt. The ocean looked worse from the bridge. The waves reached higher, the water bending and rolling below them. It took more time than she would admit, but she made it all the way up to the wheelhouse.

She was barely in the door when Lochner spoke. "Storm's only getting worse." He held the wheel and stared out the windows ahead. Calvin leaned against the panel beside him, mouth set and eyes narrowed.

"We should go back to the mainland and dock. We can wait out the storm on land," Calvin said, prepared. Obviously, they had been discussing it.

Val nodded at first, never one to argue with experts, and then she remembered the island. It was a dark mass of shadows ahead of them now, covered in clouds and rainfall. "Have you contacted the land team?"

Lochner answered first. "We've tried. No one is responding."

"They probably aren't getting the signal," Calvin explained, not one to panic or add unnecessary wood to flames—a good characteristic for a man living on a boat.

"How long would we be away?" Val asked quickly, feeling the urgency of the situation

"Hard to say," Lochner said, quick and honest. "The storm came out of nowhere. It's centered around the island, and they're on the island. It could blow over during the night, or it could last a week." He shrugged a shoulder in defeat.

Val clawed a hand through her dark hair, still damp. "Okay. Well—"

A thump quieted her, followed by another. Both Val and Calvin turned toward the door, expecting someone to walk in. Another thump, distant but dauntingly solid.

They might not have heard Maeko shouting if they hadn't all stopped to listen. It pierced the air and echoed in Val's chest, rattling her bones and washing her skin in ice.

Closest to the door, she was the first to burst out and dash down the ladder to the deck.

The boat heaved to one side, making it an uphill climb to reach Maeko where she stood at the starboard side, clinging to the railing. "What—" Val began to shout just before she followed the other woman's gaze out into the ocean. The dark shadows of sharks hovered in those churning waters. Her breath caught in her throat and not even Maeko managed to work up another scream when a ten-foot bull shark cut through the swells right for the ship, slamming headfirst into the hull. A sickly thud echoed through the vessel, and this time the whole ship shuddered just as two more sounded on the other side. She stared in shock, watching the gush of blood around the giant fish as it rolled belly-up and the waters dragged it away. Gone.

Chapter 7

"Why are they doing that?" Calvin shouted over the wind and the waves.

"I've never seen this before," Maeko yelled, and Val shook her head grimly, eyes wide to watch a great white, at least eighteen feet long, charge the ship. The hull cracked when that head hit, and her stomach lurched up into her throat.

Ed emerged from below deck, grabbing onto Calvin and shouting about hull breaches before running up the ladder to the wheelhouse. The ship was taking on water. The thudding grew more frequent until it was almost without pause. In the waves that rose around them, Val could see the cruising bodies of sharks and dolphins while yet more rushed in to spread the cracks in the hull.

The ship began to list to one side when Ed came back down from the wheelhouse. He hurried to Val, Calvin, and Maeko first. "Engine room is flooded. Captain says to prepare to speedboat if it comes to it," he shouted before hurrying off on his duties.

Calvin let out a string of curses, but before he could

make a run for the wheelhouse himself, Val grabbed his arm and pushed him toward Maeko. "Take her with you," she shouted over the storm. "Get her in a life vest!" Maeko didn't move, standing there and staring at the sharks instead. Her fingers strained her knuckles against the railing, mouth open but chest so tight that Val wasn't entirely sure the other biologist was breathing.

She left Calvin to drag Maeko up from the deck to the bridge while she practically slid across the floor to the doorway leading downstairs. She ripped the emergency bag from the wall on her way and slung it over her shoulder. Water gushed up to her knees when she came into the common area. Oliver elbowed her aside, shoving her hard into the counter before vanishing up the stairs. She'd only caught a glimpse of him but saw that he was already wearing a life vest and holding armfuls of his research and equipment.

The lights flickered when the ship began to roll. Val hugged the kitchen counter, latching on to its edges when the world turned over. Everything that wasn't bolted down went sliding or falling. Cabinet doors and drawers opened when they were highest, spilling contents everywhere. Now she knew what it would be like to be inside a snow globe. Water went everywhere, sloshing and dripping, and for one terrible moment, she was completely submerged just before everything settled against the ceiling. Val hung onto the countertop, now above, and when she let go, she fell into a pool of water dimly lit from beneath by the ceiling lamps. They flickered, the cold water completely black between those moments of light, up to her waist and rising.

She groped at the emergency kit on her shoulder, unzipping it and pulling out a flashlight. She took note of a fistful of glow sticks, a first aid kit, and an inflatable raft all packed into the bag with half a dozen more items.

"Felix!" Val shouted, turning on the flashlight to fill the dark between those flickers of light from beneath. She waded through the water, now congested with their floating belongings, toward the narrow hall of cabin doors. Her heart pounded against her throat. The water continued to rise, and the ship creaked all around her. She had to get out before it sunk, but she couldn't bring herself to leave without him.

"Felix!" she shouted his name again and was answered by the pounding of a fist against the inside of one of the cabin doors.

"Val?" Felix called, struggling to get the door to open.

She reached under the water to grab the handle. It turned, but the door didn't budge. "Together," she shouted through the thin barrier. "One. Two. Three." She pushed while he pulled, and the door popped open. Water from inside and out converged. The light from her flashlight filled the dark room. He wasn't alone.

He had one arm hooked around Poppy to pin her shoulder to his side. Together they staggered out of the cabin and into the common area. Her head lulled to the right, her eyes closed and her temple bleeding.

"Shit," Val exhaled, touching the other woman's face and trying to wake her. "Poppy. Poppy!" The water swelled up to their shoulders. They couldn't get her to wake up, and they couldn't dive with her unconscious.

Felix took the flashlight to look around the upside-down area, desperate for a way to get them out.

Val handed Poppy back to him, trading for the flashlight. "Wait here," she said before moving toward the stairs that once led up to the deck but were now under water and leading out into the open ocean.

Felix huffed out an adrenaline-infused laugh behind her. "Do I have a choice?"

She dropped down under the surface and swam out, flashing the light along the walls the whole way. Swimming out of the ship, Val grabbed onto the railing to keep from being drawn away from the boat. She skirted the sides to find their equipment still strapped to the walls where they'd left them after returning that day. Holding the flashlight with her teeth, she pulled at the ropes to let the air tanks loose, grabbing one and making sure it had a face mask before pulling it up under her arm and swimming back into the boat.

When she resurfaced, the lights inside had gone out completely. She gasped for air, her forehead touching the ceiling. She found Felix, one hand holding the leg of the table bolted down overhead and the other cradling Poppy's jaw to keep her head up. Val passed him the tank and got the mask over Poppy's face. She pulled the thin straps to make sure it was tight, the oxygen humming now that the valve was turned.

"You'll have to swim her out, but I'll lead the way," Val said, and he nodded as though they had already discussed it in detail. She could tell he was ready to get out of this boat. Val pulled the emergency bag around to her front again, no space above water to lift it but her arm reaching in to dig out a fistful of glow sticks. She cracked them all and stuffed two into the straps of Poppy's mask before setting the rest between Felix's teeth.

She gave him one last look, his cheek against the ceiling and his dark eyes watching her. She nodded once, and he nodded back before they both sunk down below the rising water. She used the flashlight to find their way out. The hall felt narrow now, and she imagined it felt even tighter

CHERYL LOW

for Felix with an oxygen tank and Poppy in his arms. As soon as they were out of the hull, Val reached back to grab Poppy's other arm. Together they swam toward the surface.

All around them, in the dying light of the afternoon, were the shapes of sharks cruising the ocean waters.

Some came close, circling as the three rose toward the surface. There were more sharks in the water that night than Val had ever seen in one place before. She regretted surfacing as soon as she had. The fear of all those predators only hit her when she couldn't see them anymore. She took a deep breath, holding Poppy's weight between herself and Felix and resisted the urge to dive back down.

Felix propelling them in one direction, the waves beating against them, pushing them under every so often. The island bobbed on the horizon ahead, dark and patient, as though it had always known they would come to it. They had no choice now. There was nowhere else to go.

The waves clapped, impossibly loud, slapping against each other in the frenzy of the storm.

Fins cut at the surface everywhere Val looked, and she felt more vulnerable in those long minutes, swimming toward an island that never seemed any closer, than she had in her whole life. It was worse than the time she was attacked—at least that shark hadn't kept her waiting, forcing her to wonder with every kick if it would be her last.

The sun went down while they swam. At one point, they were wading through debris. Plastic boxes and clothing floated in the water. They passed the reef, and suddenly the waves worked with them, pushing them toward the shoreline. Between the rising waves, she saw the shapes of other swimmers ahead, making their way toward the beach. But she forgot them when she saw Oliver drifting sedately, clinging to one of those plastic boxes on the surface.

A wave rolled over Val, pushing her under for a second. She came up, spitting water and taking a breath before letting go of Poppy. Felix looked back at her, and she pointed out Oliver before signaling him to keep moving toward the island. For a split-second, Felix looked like he might argue, but instead, he shifted Poppy against his chest and started kicking again, propelling himself backward.

Val grabbed onto the other side of the large black box, holding onto Oliver's arms where he clung to it. Together they bobbed there in the dark water. Eventually they might get to land like this, but eventually wouldn't be soon enough. He looked bad—paper pale, nearly transparent, skin thin and hanging on his bones. Dark bags hung under his eyes, and she wondered if he'd been hit with something when the boat rolled. From the look of him, she might have believed it had been days since she saw him last.

"Oliver," Val called his name, loud enough to be heard over the storm.

At first, he didn't look back at her, his gaze blank and fixed in the waters behind her.

"Oliver," she said his name again, louder, her fingers digging into his arms.

He blinked, and his lips parted, dragging in a breath. She looked back at the island. It was still a long swim off. Oliver started to mumble, and she looked at him again, weighing her options. He was in shock. If he stayed disconnected like this, she could swim him to shore, but if he turned violent or panicked, he could easily drown them both.

"Oliver. Come on," she pleaded, holding onto his arms still. "We're close. It's only a little farther to the island."

He looked at her then, his blue eyes like glass with only darkness beneath. "There is no island," he whispered, voice shredded. "There is only death." He shook his head, tears slipping from his eyes to roll down his cheeks.

She felt the moment he let go and saw it in those haunted eyes. His body relaxed, and his fingers released the box between them. Val grappled with his sleeves to hang onto him, the box slipping out from between them, bobbing low before bursting out to the side. She went under with him, the water so dark now that it was little more than ink. She kicked hard to push them both above the surface again, taking deep breaths and holding his back against her chest. He didn't fight her, and she didn't try talking to him anymore. She didn't have to bother with reason if he didn't struggle. She held his jaw to keep his face above the water and started kicking, pushing them toward the beach. With her back to the island, all she could watch was the dark ocean, every so often seeing or feeling a shark drift by. So close and there was nothing she could do if they decided to make a meal of them.

She started to cry when she realized how light Oliver was, when she kicked and kicked and never felt his legs in her way. She couldn't see the blood they trailed in the water, but she could see and hear the sharks following them, splashing at the surface. A part of her begged to let him go—to swim faster and get away, but that part couldn't convince her arms. She looked back at the island as they got closer and closer. Felix was there in the waves that crashed against the sand, coming back out into the water to meet her. Lochner came out as well, and she finally let go of Oliver when they took him from her.

Val cried harder and let the waves shove her onto the sand, clawing at the wet ground to drag herself onto the beach. She rolled onto her side to watch the two men carry Oliver out of the water, and everyone finally saw what she had already realized.

Maeko screamed from where she sat on the beach with Poppy in her lap.

Oliver was dead. Half his body had been eaten. The base of his sternum stuck out of his abdomen, bright white in the night. Muscles with shredded jacket and flesh hung loosely from his torso, dangling like too much wet hair. Felix and Lochner put him down at the edge of the waves, and the tendrils of his intestines rolled against the surf in place of his legs.

Calvin grabbed Val under the arms and pulled her up the beach, away from the water. He sat her down and then knelt in front of her in the sand. "Are you all right?" he asked, voice sober and heavy. She blinked back at him, realizing that he was doing to her now what she had been doing to Oliver on that floating box in the water. He was trying to decide if she was in shock.

Val swallowed hard and nodded. She scrubbed her wrists against her eye sockets. It was just a reflex to push away tears; it didn't really matter because she was drenched. "Poppy?" she croaked out, looking past his shoulder to the other two women.

"She's awake. She hit her head pretty bad, but the cut is small," Calvin assured.

Val nodded again, looking around the dark beach. Poppy was now soothing Maeko instead of the other way around. Lochner and Felix came to stand over them. There wasn't much anyone could say to make Maeko feel better. There was no reason for any of them to feel better right now. Oliver was dead. The Charlene had sunk, and they were stuck on an abandoned island.

"Ed?" Val asked when she realized the first mate of the ship was missing from their collective.

Calvin sat down next to her, his back to the ocean.

She turned her head to look at him. He didn't look back, watching the dark jungle instead. "Oliver freaked out and got onto the speedboat with Ed. Ed wanted to wait for the rest of us, but Oliver didn't. They scuffled and—" He swallowed hard, and his jaw flexed against whatever emotion knotted in his chest. "Oliver pushed Ed overboard. He hit his head against the ship and started to sink, so I jumped out to get him. When I came up, Oliver was driving away from the wreck." He shook his head more to himself than to her. "Ed didn't make it to shore." There was something dark hanging in his words, something in the way he said it. It left her certain that Ed had not died quietly.

She looked at Oliver's corpse again—what was left of it—and couldn't stop herself from wondering if there was anything left of Ed's.

Chapter 8

Almost a half hour slipped by in relative silence. The storm moved out to sea and left them to dry out in the dark.

"What do we do?" Poppy broke the quiet with a whisper.

"We have to find Julie and Zach," Val replied, throat raw. "They'll have a radio and an emergency beacon."

"Not to mention gear," Calvin added.

"W-we're going in there?" Maeko asked loudly, pointing at the trees that were little more than shapes of shadows in the night. "No. No." She shook her head firmly. She'd been standing for the last twenty minutes, arms wrapped tightly around herself, squeezing the saltwater from her sweater. It was, perhaps, their only blessing that Isla de los Perdidos was a tropical island. Even at night, the humid air warmed their skin.

"We'll wait until morning," Felix assured her before he took a deep breath and then let it out, looking to Val and Calvin where they sat just a few feet away. "But we should move down the beach for the night. We can huddle together until dawn."

"Move? Why?" Poppy asked, confused.

Lochner nodded. "The land team was moving that way." He pointed down the left side of the beach. "We might as well move that way too tonight."

"Why do we have to move?" Maeko asked, shifting nervously on her feet.

Val and Calvin got up, and Felix offered Poppy a hand. Maeko asked again, and Calvin sighed, taking the flashlight from Val and turning it on. He let it shine briefly over the waves and Oliver's body. Already there were ghost crabs in the surf with him. The light moved past him to the beach; eyes glinted back like flares in the surf, and the crocodiles hissed at being exposed.

Maeko let out a mess of sounds, all catching in her throat and overflowing her lips. She moved closer to the others, grabbing at Poppy's arm but still shaking her head. "N-no. You're going to leave him here?" Her voice grew shrill with disbelief.

Calvin turned the light in the other direction down the beach, making note of any predators in their way. If they moved together as a group and gave the crocodiles enough room, they would be fine. They wanted the easy meal. And that's what Oliver was now. Not a person or a colleague— but a meal for this island.

"They're right, Maeko," Val whispered, reaching out for the other woman's arm. "We should move."

Maeko shook her head hard, eyes large with tears. "We should bury him."

Val let out an exhausted, miserable sigh that scraped at her throat, leaving it sore. "And are you going to dig the hole? Deep enough to keep animals from digging him back up? Or are you going to keep the crocodiles back while we dig it?" She shook her head, licking her lips because she immediately regretted how hard those words sounded when they came out. "We need to move. We'll wait out the night, and then we'll follow the land team's path to catch up."

Felix came up beside Maeko, rubbing her arms to gently push her to start walking in the same direction the others were already shifting in. Poppy wrapped an arm around her waist to hug her to her side, taking her signals from Felix to get Maeko moving.

"Julie and Zach have an emergency beacon," Poppy reminded her in a gentle voice. "We'll push it and have a whole rescue team here."

Maeko cried loudly, but she was walking, and that was all they could ask at the moment. Together, the six of them moved down the coastline. Calvin and Lochner led the way, avoiding the monsters in the dark to find them a new spot on dry sand along a wide stretch of the beach. They were all a little grateful for Maeko's sobs and Poppy's soothing words if only to drown out the sound of fighting crocodiles behind them.

Val and Felix walked at the back of the small traveling party, keeping Maeko and Poppy within arm's reach. "You're all right?" he whispered, and it took Val a moment to realize it was a question rather than an assurance.

She nodded, eyes and heart tired. "I will be when we get off this island."

Felix took her hand in his, squeezing gently. "Oh, *mi sol*, that might be a couple days." He whispered carefully so that Maeko didn't hear.

Val nodded grimly. They were two days behind Julie and the others, but they would be able to cover more ground since they wouldn't be stopping to film or explore along the way. Val had no interest in what this island hid beneath the lush greens of its jungle. She was going to find her sister and that emergency beacon and get the hell out of here.

Not long after they found a spot to wait out the night and convinced Maeko to sit down, she fell asleep. Val and Poppy sat with their backs to each other for support. Calvin and Lochner talked in low voices, Calvin leaned into Lochner's arms, with both men facing down the other end of the beach to keep watch. Val stared down what now felt like her length of evening beach. The clouds shifted away from the island, and the moon lit up the edge of thick trees. The water shone black, rolling up and down the blue sand. It was as though the waves were reaching, stretching out each time, desperate to invade those trees.

Val fell asleep in intervals, always waking with the irritating certainty that she hadn't slept at all. In the last fluttering of her lashes, before sinking into deep sleep, she imagined someone standing in those trees. He was thin and tall and nothing but a shadow. He stood with his toes touching the sand and his eyes watching the surf. He watched it with a will to make it slither back from the trees, and the waves watched him in return, reaching with more eagerness—desperate to wet his toes.

Chapter 9

Morning came, and the storm passed. For a moment, sitting there on the beach, her clothes dry and the rising sun sending streams of new color across the sky, it was as though the night before hadn't happened. And for that moment she was alone, sitting on a beautiful beach looking out at the ocean. And then she felt the back against hers shift as Poppy woke.

"What time is it?" the other woman asked, voice raspy with sleep.

Val turned her wrist and looked down at her watch. She stared at the unmoving second hand. She'd gone swimming with this watch a thousand times. It had never stopped before. Never. Her heart sank, but she looked away before she could feel the edges of despair so eager to press in at her. "It doesn't matter, Poppy. It's morning."

Val looked around. Lochner was awake and watching the trees, but Calvin still slept curled in the larger man's lap. Felix leaned against Val's side, his neck bent and his chest rising and falling evenly. Poppy moved, taking her warmth with Val's when she stood and stretched.

For a moment, Val just watched Felix sleep, wishing she didn't have to wake him. It wasn't until she started to move, body turning toward his to catch him if he fell, that she realized he was holding her hand. She looked down at their entangled fingers against the sand. Back when they were together, before she left, they used to sleep like that—holding hands. She had told him about how otters held hands when they slept so that they wouldn't drift apart from one another, and he had smiled brightly and called her his "significant otter."

She squeezed his hand and kissed his cheek, her face nuzzled in under his. "Wake up." It sounded apologetic, probably because she had nothing but a hard day to offer him.

Felix woke easily. Maeko was a lot more difficult. She wasn't asleep, but she didn't want to get up. She didn't want to go into the woods. She wanted to wait on the beach for a rescue, staring at the horizon as though one was on its way.

After what felt like an hour of arguing, Val started walking. "Fine! Wait on the beach, alone, in the dark," she called over her shoulder. "Because it'll be at least two days before we get back to you!"

Calvin immediately liked this decision and followed her. Poppy tugged at Maeko's hand. She was sympathetic to Maeko's terror but drawn, as though by gravity, to follow the others.

Lochner and Felix lingered long enough in between to be sure that Maeko and Poppy weren't left behind. Val led the way through the trees and over the thickly rooted terrain. She had studied the map and been there when Julie and Zach went over their travel plans.

They walked most of the morning in silence. Daylight

filtered down through the thick leaves of the trees high above, vines and saplings crowding every space in between. There was endless sound in every direction: the rustling of leaves, the dropping of nuts, and the breaking of twigs. A constant, erratic melody of birds and bugs sang out to the daytime life of the jungle. Every so often, Val reached out to run fingers along a tree, touching the blaze Zach had cut into the wood on either side of their trail as they'd ventured deeper and deeper inland.

Calvin and Val maintained the lead while Lochner and Felix stayed behind Maeko and Poppy. It wasn't something they planned or discussed, but Val understood why Felix and the captain fell to the rear. They were all unsure just how long Maeko was going to keep walking before deciding it was too much. They couldn't risk losing someone in the jungle. If they fell off their path, they might never find it again.

"How long before we catch up with them?" Poppy broke hours of silence. Honestly, Val was more disturbed by just how long the usually chatty woman had gone without talking.

"Maybe tomorrow," Felix answered, optimistic as ever, but it was the same idea Val pushed toward. The land team had two days on them. They would be moving toward their third campsite today if they were on schedule. Val hoped they weren't. She hoped that the storm had delayed them. Maybe they had stay in the same spot for two nights. Maybe they would catch up to them tomorrow if they pushed hard. It still meant one more night in the dark, without gear, without food or water or fire or tents. No one wanted to point that out.

It was almost midday and sticky humid. Val rubbed sweat from her forehead, but it felt pointless. She'd taken off her sweater hours ago and tied it around her waist. It was hard to resist the urge to ditch it in that heat, but she knew the night wouldn't be as hot.

Calvin carried their only flashlight, the base stuffed into the back pocket of his jeans.

"Should we rest soon?" Poppy asked, probably just trying to stave off the silence of their march through the trees with a little more chatter.

"Why?" Calvin snapped, tired and unamused. Val could almost hear his thoughts on the matter. Why stop if they didn't have anything to eat or drink? Why put more distance between themselves and that emergency beacon?

Felix spoke up from behind them. "We should keep an eye out for a stream or creak."

Val brushed her thumb over another score mark on a tree.

"I'm thirsty," Maeko mumbled bitterly, as though his suggestion had been a cruel reminder.

They trudged through the glossy foliage for a while longer. Val found herself trying to think of something to say just to lighten the gloom building in Calvin beside her or maybe alleviate the tension gathering around Poppy. She had known the younger woman for years and had taken part in countless conversations with her, and yet she couldn't think of a single thing to say.

As though he read her mind, Felix broke the quiet of the group. "Hey, Cal," he called up toward the front.

Calvin grunted in reply but didn't miss a step or look back.

"Did Val ever tell you how we met?"

Val looked back over her shoulder to shoot her husband a glare past Poppy and Maeko.

Calvin shrugged. His t-shirt had dried out the night before but was now sweat-stained and clinging to him again. "Yeah. She was your shark guide." He didn't sound the least bit amused.

"No." Felix shook his head, smiling. "We met the night before—"

"Felix..." Val warned, more on reflex than anything else. Yes, it was an embarrassing story, but they were ship-wrecked and that put things into perspective.

"I'd been in New Zealand rafting. They have these amaz-ing rapids. And afterward, I went over to Australia thinking I could see crocodiles. Turns out they don't like you to see them outside the zoos so much. So, I went to Perth thinking I'd at least do some surfing before I went back to Brazil." He paused to step over a fallen branch and then duck under another, following the rest of them. "The night I ran into Val was the day before my flight home. She was in this bar—"

"Felix, really..." Val called back, now a few steps ahead of Calvin. He'd slowed down just a little when the story got his interest.

"She was drunk. Completely, black-out drunk," Felix said, smiling fondly around the words. "She'd lost funding for her study and, I guess, lost her mind." He laughed; it sounded beautiful even on a day as bad as this one. They'd agreed to leave this part out of their meet-cute, but under the circumstances, she couldn't exactly muster the will to be angry, not really. "She was doing Jägerbombs and calling this guy at the bar 'grandma'."

Calvin made an odd sound, and Val looked back, wor-ried he might have tripped until she realized he was trying hard not to laugh. He didn't like being tricked out of his sulk, and as long as his back was to Felix and he swallowed down his amusement, he could still pretend.

"You weren't exactly an angel yourself," Val called back, deciding that this line of rambling storytelling was probably the best they could do for each other right now. "Didn't you buy me some of those drinks?"

"I had to," Felix countered. "You were broke."

Poppy giggled.

"I was fine."

"When the bar closed, she decided she was going to the beach. It was only a couple blocks away."

"Felix." Val raised her voice, but it was all for show now. He was going to tell it, and she wasn't going to stop him.

"She stripped down, rambling about the amazing sharks in those waters. She was giving me a lecture about bull sharks, stark naked on the beach. I was trying to talk her out of going in—I mean, I'm no expert, but she was drunk, and everyone has seen the opening of *Jaws*."

"Did she go in?" Poppy asked.

Val bit her lip and shook her head, ducking to the side out of the way of a low vine.

"Nah. She didn't. Because she barfed all over herself and then immediately passed out. Immediately. Mouth still open and body curled from heaving up all that Jäger. She went down so fast I was afraid she'd died."

Poppy and Calvin laughed. Calvin was the only one trying not to, rubbing the back of his hand over his mouth as though to wipe away those sounds.

"I took her to my hotel room, cleaned her up, and put her to bed. In the morning, I told her she'd promised to take me out to see sharks and that we'd already made a deal about the price. Not sure why, but she always wants to skip that part of the story."

Val sighed. "And thank you so much for keeping it to yourself," she complained halfheartedly, looking up to watch two red macaws in the trees. She realized quickly that there were more. At least twenty all the way up, like great big flowers on the branches. Those feathers could be worth a small fortune for the cold-hearted or the desperate.

Her steps picked up when the ground slanted down. The air grew noticeably cooler, and the sound of moving water hit her eardrums like a siren calling out for attention. She stopped sloppily, almost tripping. Calvin grabbed her arm to make sure she didn't, his face scrunching for half a second to look at her before he heard it, too. "Don't lose the path," he said, voice low and urgent. Calvin wasn't going to lose his head over water no matter how thirsty he was. She could feel it in his presence at her side. He was going to get off this island.

Val nodded. "I'll follow the blaze marks, you keep an eye out for the stream," she decided, and he agreed quickly.

"Loch," Calvin called back. "We hear water. We'll find it, but everyone stay together," he said to his husband, but the commanding tone was obviously meant for everyone else. Loch grunted in reply and kept an eye on Maeko.

They continued to follow the trail, the sound growing louder until they could see the split in the trees and the meter-wide stream rolling right across their path. A collective sigh of relief stole through them and, for the first time since that morning, they fell out of their marching order. It was a beautiful sight and not just because they were so desperately thirsty. The water sparkled in the light that bore down from the trees, moving quickly over rocks and soft land.

Calvin reached it first, crouching down and cupping his hand to lift a mouthful. He drank and then hummed in confirmation that it wasn't salt. He put his hands to the stones along the edge and leaned down, pushing his face in and drinking.

Val walked through the stream—it wasn't even up to her knees—and found the next blazed tree on their path. She tied her sweater around it, a bright blue flag in a sea of green to remind them where they'd been if they strayed along the water.

Poppy sat down. She drank first and then finally turned and flopped back into the shallow stream. Both Calvin and Felix jumped when she splashed. Calvin shot her a hard look for her behavior, but Val couldn't help but wonder if he wasn't jealous she'd done it first.

"Go downstream if you're going to swim in it," Calvin berated, getting up and going upstream from her.

Poppy splashed him but quickly looked away when he turned toward her again.

Val returned to them and the water, still the only one on the other side of the stream, when she noticed that Lochner hadn't approached. He stood at the edge of the trees, a few meters behind Maeko. His skin was red from the heat and his shirt wet with sweat, but he didn't leave his post to find comfort in the cool waters. His arms crossed his chest tightly with his sweater slung over one surprisingly beefy shoulder.

"Maeko," Val called to get the other marine biologist's attention. Her dark eyes snapped up from the others at the stream to look across it at Val. "Come over here." She waved her closer.

Lochner unfolded his arms when the woman walked around the group and through the water beside Poppy. He followed her forward but stopped at the stream, stooping to drink and rest.

"It could be full of parasites," Maeko complained, skeptical but thirsty, eyes fixed on the water.

Felix swallowed a mouthful and then laughed. "I don't know about you, but I've been shot up with just about every inoculation on this planet, and if I get a parasite or something new, then I'll get that dealt with when we get home." He lifted a handful of water to wet his face.

Val nodded and touched Maeko's back, urging her closer to the water again. "Better to have a parasite to deal with later than dehydration now." She smiled gently. "Just think how nice a hospital will be after this. Like a five-star resort."

Poppy laughed, still lounging in the water.

Maeko let out a heaving breath when she gave in, sitting down by the stream. She brought up handfuls to wash her face and arms, cooling her skin before finally giving in to her thirst and drinking. Once she'd taken a sip from her palm, she gave up resisting. She leaned down and drank deep.

Val almost regretted sitting, certain that she'd never want to get up again. Poppy hummed a song, familiar but not something Val could place. They sat by the stream for at least twenty minutes before Felix got up and stretched. "I'm going to look for the little boy's room. No one leave me behind," he said casually.

Calvin jumped up. "Me, too." He followed Felix downstream from the group, down a hill and into the trees.

When Val felt almost sick on water, she took one more big gulp and then sat back. She looked up at the flutter of wings to watch those scarlet macaws follow them, gliding from branch to branch until they were shifting about in the treetops above the traveling party. They spread their wings and beat at the air, tugging at the branches they held in their talons before letting go, bouncing in what looked like amusement.

Poppy whistled at them, and one cawed back.

Maeko appeared too tired to feign interest in birds. "We left him," she mumbled.

Poppy stopped whistling, head swiveling toward the other woman, sadness seeping back into her expression.

"We just left him on the beach," Maeko repeated, staring at the water.

Val took a deep breath and stood up. "He wasn't alive," she said clearly, hating the way Maeko made it sound. They hadn't abandoned him. They hadn't left him to die. She swam him to shore herself. Oliver was already dead when they reached the beach. He was half a body when they walked away from him. "We had no choice."

"We should have buried him."

"Why?" Val demanded, voice rising. She didn't like where this was going or where it put her. She didn't want to be the cold one. She didn't want to be harsh.

Maeko stood up, too, suddenly not okay with having to look up at Val. "It would have been the right thing to do!" she shouted back, hands balled into fists. "But you just left him there, and now we're hiking through the woods like it's nothing!"

Poppy crawled out of the stream to stand on the same side as Val, her t-shirt and shorts dripping. She pretended rather poorly not to hear the conversation turned argument, her shoes squishing wetly.

"We are not safe," Val said finally.

Maeko and Poppy both looked at her then. She felt Lochner watching them all. "We are shipwrecked on an island no one visits," Val continued. She'd tried to avoid saying these things since they first reached the beach. She thought maybe if they kept things light, they could get through this and grieve when they were finally off the island. "We have no gear. No supplies. No food. And we are at least two, probably three, days behind my sister and the others."

Maeko took a step back as though she'd been hit, eyes clear and sober. She twisted where she stood to look a-round at the jungle anew.

"We couldn't bury Oliver," Lochner said firmly from be-side them, confirming the decision again.

"All of our energy now has to go toward surviving and finding the land team. That's it, Maeko. That's all we can do. Grieving won't help you right now. It won't help any of us. So yeah, we make conversation if we can because it might help to keep us moving. This is going to get hard-er before it gets better," Val promised grimly.

Maeko opened her mouth to reply, but whatever words she gathered died in her chest, swallowed up by too many terrible truths.

Poppy was quick to try to change the mood, bouncing from one wet sneaker to the other. "I don't know about you two, but I have to pee. Anyone want to come with and keep an eye out for snakes for me?" she said in an urgent tone. Her long lashes, still wet from the stream, batted at the other two women pleadingly.

Maeko nodded again, sullen now. Poppy held out a hand, and Maeko took it.

"Don't go far," Lochner said, watching their direction into the trees.

Val took a deep breath and then let it out slowly. Loch-ner was looking back at her from where he stood on the other side of the water, beneath the macaws.

"Does that make us tinkle buddies?" she asked, pulling up a smile.

Lochner's beard twitched in such a way that she was

sure he smiled back. "I don't know about you, but I don't need privacy to piss," he said, turning his back to her and facing the nearest tree. He unzipped his pants and gave a little hop to take himself out and another breath before he started to make mud of the dirt at the base of that tree.

Val let out a laugh just as Felix and Calvin returned.

"Where's Poppy and Maeko?" Felix asked, and the tone of his voice and the look on his face stole away her moment of amusement.

Val watched both men carefully, seeing the gravity of their expressions only now that they stood close by. "Ladies' room," she said. "What is it?"

They looked at each other before Felix held out a hand toward her and Calvin walked away.

She crossed the stream and took Felix's palm, her forehead pinching with too many questions.

Calvin went to Lochner, standing closer and whispering. She couldn't divine any answers from Lochner's steely expression, and soon enough Felix led her out of site. They walked in the same direction Calvin and Felix had gone when they left to take a piss, only this time they didn't slip off into the trees.

Felix walked her downstream. She was about to ask again what was wrong when she saw it. A large body lying in the water. Val jerked to a stop so quickly that her bones hurt in reply; his hand held hers tightly and pulled her forward. She stumbled a little on the muddy bank before they both came to a stop.

At first, she didn't get any closer, still standing behind his arm and staring at the creature. Finally, Val let go of his fingers and took those last steps to look down at the jaguar. It was dead. Body dropped across the stream as though it had keeled over while taking a drink, lurching forward to collapse on the water. She leaned closer. The big cat's tongue hung out of its mouth, thick with old blood and flies. The blood looked black and matted the fur below its eyes.

"What the hell?"

"Calvin said it's been dead at least a day or two."

She looked up at him. "And nothing has eaten it or dragged it off?"

"Maybe it was the only predator in the area? Jaguars have territory, right?" Felix offered his thoughts, and from the easy sound of them, she'd guess that he'd already gone over this with Calvin.

He came closer and reached out to point at some of the markings on the coat of the cat. Not the usual spots, but muddy little cloves mostly washed away by the storm. "Brocket tracks," he said, and she looked at him with a raised eyebrow.

"Brocket?"

"It's a small deer," Felix explained before pointing to the muddy bank on either side. There, in the ground, were tiny hoof prints that had sunk deep enough to survive the night, collecting little pools of murky water.

She felt her face scrunching even more in confusion. "A deer walked over a dead jaguar?"

Felix shrugged, looking uncomfortable with the oddity. "Calvin wasn't sure what had killed it either. It's bleeding from the eyes, ears, and mouth."

Val stood upright and took a step back, suddenly wishing she hadn't been as close as she had. "Some kind of illness?"

Felix shrugged again. "We thought you should see it. Calvin's going to let Loch know, but maybe..." He trailed, unsure.

Val already nodded. "We shouldn't mention it to Maeko and Poppy." She took a couple more steps back from the dead cat before turning away. "I'm not sure what would be more upsetting to them, its mysterious death or the fact that there are jaguars in this jungle." She scrubbed a hand over her face. "I hate land."

Felix caught up with her, his arm curling around her shoulders on the way back to the others. "To be fair, the ocean wasn't treating us great either."

She let out a huff of agreement that felt more like defeat.

Chapter 10

When they got back to the group, everyone was standing between the bank of the stream and the tree she'd tied her blue sweater to. Val pulled at the sleeves to get it loose and then shook it out in case anything had crawled off the bark to look for a new home. She'd spent enough time with Julie in jungles to pick up a few tricks—just enough to be able to say she'd learned from her mistakes.

"All right." Calvin broke the silence and stretched out an arm toward the unknown, offering Val the lead again. "Ladies first."

Lochner coughed at that, but Val ignored him and set about the task of finding their path again. Like before, both she and Calvin kept to the front to watch for the next blazed tree in the trail. Maeko and Poppy made up the middle, and Felix and Lochner trailed behind.

It didn't take long for them to fall back into silence, or rather, to have all of their own moving sounds swallowed up by the constant noise of the jungle around them. Val felt certain that it would never be silent again, not here anyway.

"How did you and Loch meet?" She broke some of the quiet, looking for a distraction.

Calvin's brow pinched, jaw tipping toward her in confusion before smiling a little and returning the bulk of his attention to their trail. "Singles website."

Val barked out a laugh. "Liar."

"It's true," he persisted. "'Boat captain seeks hot guy that loves to swim.'"

Poppy laughed behind them, picking up her steps to get closer to the conversation. "Really?"

"Sure," Calvin lied.

"No." Val shook her head as she found the next tree. They were moving uphill now, every step more work, but she knew that it would lead to a plateau. She'd seen it on the maps. They were getting close to the first campsite. A part of her couldn't help but hope Julie would still be there, that the rain had somehow delayed them the whole of yesterday, and maybe their gear had been damaged and they decided to stay put today, too. It was a stupid hope. Their gear was made to survive a monsoon.

She found herself hoping for worse things. Maybe one of their camera crew got hurt. Nothing serious. A twisted ankle? A broken arm? Val had never hoped for anyone to be injured before, but trudging up that incline, she'd wish a lot worse than a broken arm on someone she didn't know if it would put her sister sitting safely at that first campsite with her emergency beacon in hand.

"How did you really meet?" Poppy pressed Calvin.

"Swim class," he lied again, smiling to himself.

Val looked at him sideways, unable to hide her own grin. "Really? So, you were both there with yellow floaties on, and it was love at first dive?"

Calvin coughed out a laugh. "No. No. He had a life vest

on, and my floaties were blue with ducks."

Poppy giggled. "I don't believe you."

Calvin looked back, faking offense before pushing on. Slowly the ground evened out again, the trees not quite as tight anymore and the grass tall. For the first time in what felt like the whole day, they could really see the sky. Bright blue in every direction, giving way to horizons of treetops.

They looked skyward, and the sun looked back, merciless as always. Val was well acquainted with the cruelty of the sun and the whims of the weather, but she always preferred to endure it at sea. She was sweaty and sticky, and before the treetops cleared into open sky, she'd been fighting back a strong sense of claustrophobia. Was that a thing? Could she be claustrophobic, moving freely through a jungle? The air was so wet and thick—why not?

She began to slow, crossing that field toward the next line of trees, just to prolong her time under the bright blue sky. Maybe, if she tipped her head back and looked up through her lashes, she could pretend she was floating in the water. The grass whipped at her knees, reminding her that she wasn't. In fact, every step she took carried her farther and farther from the shore, toward the peak, toward Julie.

Julie. There was a breath of hope in that name when it cut across her thoughts. She dropped her head forward again and picked up her pace just before Poppy would have bumped into her. Julie would know what to do in the jungle —she always did. This was her place, and Zach would have a dozen emergency plans ready to put into action. She just had to get to them.

They were about to slip into the next row of trees when she saw it, an object hanging from a branch high above.

"Do you see that?" Calvin asked, stopping and bringing

a hand up to cup his brow, shielding his gaze from the sun to squint at the black plastic dangling by a strap from the green canopy.

Val took a few more steps toward it. "It's a camera," she announced.

Poppy and Felix picked up their pace, hurrying through the long grass, heads tipped back, trying to get a closer look. "I think it's one of ours," Felix said. "But what the hell is it doing up there?"

The rest joined them at the base of the tall tree.

"I can climb it if someone gives me a boost to that branch," Calvin said, pointing out the lowest one, still well above their reach. The wide base of the tree, coated with smooth bark, offered little help for climbing.

Felix nodded and laced his fingers together, opening his palms and positioning himself beneath the nearest branch.

Lifting both hands up over her brow, Val blocked the sun from her gaze, looking up. She stood under the camera in case the shaking of the tree knocked it loose. Calvin got a hold of the lowest branch and used it to hoist himself upward, getting on top of it, and from there climbing higher.

Standing under the camera, Val could see bright orange in the tree above it. Her eyes widened when she recognized the shape of shoulders and realized that it was the back of a hoodie. "Megan?" she called, voice loud. The others turned to look at her first before hurrying closer to follow her gaze up into the treetops. That hunched back shuddered, head bent forward and out of sight. Her legs dangled over the other side, canopied in thick leaves and a nest of branches.

"Megan?" Poppy shouted, worry thick in her voice.

Calvin perched on a branch on the other side of the tree. He grabbed the camera first, pulling it loose and tossing it down to Val before trying to look around the tree. "Is she there?" He sounded skeptical.

"She's sitting on a branch on the other side. Up higher," Felix explained, and Calvin looked around, trying to figure out how to get up to her.

"Megan, are you hurt?" Poppy called.

Megan twitched, jostling against the branches. Felix moved closer, arms loose and ready to try to catch her if she fell.

Calvin hugged the tree, his shoes scraping against the bark when he clung to it, and squirmed his way around.

"Careful," Lochner warned, following him from the ground, skirting the trunk.

Megan shuddered.

Calvin reached.

He grabbed onto the branch she sat on, beside her thigh, and started to lift himself. He had one arm hooked around it when he reached up and touched her back. Without warning, Megan fell. Poppy gasped, and Felix tensed, arms out, but she didn't fall out of the tree. Her legs were caught in the branches, her torso and arms dropping back to dangle upside down. Her dirty blonde hair swayed limp and wet in the air.

Her eyes were open, but all color had drained into a glassy, milky film. Her face was stretched in a scream that no longer had breath, teeth bright and lips drawn back. A hole had been carved in her chest through the torn material of her shirt. The cavity stretched from between her breasts down below her navel. Bones gleamed between meat, and broken ribs dangled by sinew that still held them to the body.

Maeko screamed, and a large monkey perched in Megan's lap looked up. Those black eyes fixed on Calvin, so close. Greedy, little hands grabbed at Megan's corpse as the monkey leaned over it, mouth gaping to howl at the intruder. The sound was deafening, that dark face splitting to expose long, white teeth gleaming in sticky red.

Calvin practically pushed himself back, letting go of the branch and falling.

The treetops exploded with movement. Dozens of large, hairy, black bodies shifted among the leaves, moving closer to scream down at them.

Lochner broke Calvin's fall the best he could, both men landing hard on the grass before picking themselves up, urged on by those horrible howls and the dead body of the girl in the tree, now swaying as the monkey on her legs jumped and screamed down at them.

Val stood there, frozen. She held the camera to her chest and stared up at the howler monkey. She had seen them before with Julie. They were loud, keeping territory limits by the distance their sound could travel. They weren't meat eaters. She stared into that mouth, bits of flesh caught between finger-long teeth and gore sticking to the fur of its face. It certainly looked like a meat eater today.

Felix grabbed her by the arm and pulled. Maeko had been the first to run, and Poppy chased after her. After that, running looked like a good idea, but Calvin had been the one with the sense to get ahead and grab Maeko's elbow. He pulled them in the direction their trail had been. They ran hard and far, and Val wished she'd had the sense to stop and look for the next tree in their path, but adrenaline had driven them to put as much distance as possible between themselves and the howlers.

They stopped running when the sound became distant,

far away in the trees and melting into the edges of other sounds, into the hum of bugs and the squawk of birds. Panting, they stood in the jungle, no one willing to be the first to speak. Maeko sobbed and shook her head, and Val gripped the camera, pushing the shape of the lens against her ribs.

Sound and vision slip away. Megan was dead. Not just dead, but in a tree being eaten by non-carnivorous monkeys. Her breathing grew rapid, her shoulders shaking. Julie. Julie was in this jungle somewhere. She wouldn't have left someone from her team behind like that. Something had happened.

What if they were all dead?

What if Julie was dead?

Her breath caught in her throat, hand flying to her mouth to push back the cry that wanted so desperately to escape. What if Julie was dead and they were looking for corpses?

Chapter 11

Hands grabbed onto her shoulders, pressing warm fingers against her muscles and shaking her. She blinked until her vision cleared. Felix stared at her with his dark eyes, glassy with tears. Sweat beaded against his temple, rolling down to his jaw. His lips parted, dragging at ragged breaths. He looked the same as he had that day when she lay on the deck bleeding out, staring up at him.

"She's not dead," he said firmly as though he'd read her thoughts. Or had she been talking out loud? "Julie's not dead. The plan is the same."

She stared back at him for another minute before nodding firmly, gathering herself enough to finally look around. Poppy sat on the ground, arms wrapped around her legs and forehead to her knees. She cried hard, shaking her head and choking on her words. Felix left Val to soothe the other woman, rubbing her back. "We're going to be all right." He spoke to Poppy in that deep, reassuring voice. "It's going to be all right," he lied, and Val was glad he did. Someone had to.

Val started turning around and around, looking at the

trees. "Fuck."

Calvin and Lochner heard her, and Calvin hurried to help her look for another tree along the trail Julie and Zach had left. Had they lost it, or had the land team stopped marking trees? No. They had at least made it to the first camp that first day. Val replayed her conversation with Julie over and over. The radio crackling, people talking in the background. They had made it to the prison and the first campsite. They had settled in. She had been so happy.

Val and Calvin searched, straying from one another, heads whipping back every so often just to make sure they hadn't lost the group.

"I can't find anything," Calvin shouted, an edge of anger grating his words.

Val was about to reply in frustration when she made out a shape in the vegetation ahead. A wall, half crumbled and coated in creeping vines. A building in the jungle. Her heart slammed against her ribs, and she nodded to no one but herself and her desperation. The prison.

"This way!" Val called loudly and turned around to wave the others to her.

Lochner had Maeko over his shoulder like a mumbling sack of potatoes, and Val decided not to ask about it. Maeko didn't seem to notice that she was being carried. She wasn't exactly crying. She mumbled in Japanese, her eyes wide but unseeing, and all color drained from her face.

Felix had talked Poppy onto her feet, and the other woman was nodding, pushing through the greens ahead of him now.

Calvin reached Val first, brow pinched and gaze scrutinizing the old building mostly swallowed by jungle fauna. "What is it?"

She hesitated to say but realized they'd figure it out

soon enough. "There were a few different settlement attempts on Isla de los Perdidos," Val explained, walking quickly down a slope. She had to take it sideways, one hand skimming the ground to keep her balance. "This was one of them. They meant for it to be a prison—you know, on an island so no one gets away. It didn't work out, though. I think it was only in use for half a year." She tried to skim over the story so it didn't sound like what it was— an abandoned prison on an island rumored to be haunted.

"You're kidding," Felix mumbled, keeping to the back of their traveling party.

"Julie and Zach were going to make camp nearby on the first night. We can use it for shelter tonight and catch up with them tomorrow," Val pressed, clinging to that original plan now and pretending nothing had changed. But everything had changed. Something had gone wrong with the land team. They could be anywhere. They could be dead.

They came upon the old prison, one wall broken and an iron door standing without a frame. Thick roots and vines had overtaken the former fortress, and thin trees stuck up out of it where the roofing had collapsed. They could have gone in through that broken entrance, but Val decided to keep walking along the side of the building. She told herself it was so the others could get used to the idea, but really it was for her. She was afraid of what she'd find, remembering Megan dangling from that tree.

"We still have at least another hour or two of daylight," Val continued because no one else had taken up talking yet. "Calvin and I can take a look around for the campsite and see if they left anything behind." Her heart felt heavy in her chest, weighing down her shoulders. Would they still be at the campsite? Would their belongings? Would she find Julie in the same condition as Megan?

She swallowed hard and pushed those fears down deep in her gut. "We'll be able to pick up the trail when we find their site." She came to a stop on the other end of the pale brick wall. The entrance on this side was somewhat more welcoming and less dilapidated. A young tree had grown right against the threshold, pinning one door open.

Val hesitated, considering her traveling party. Should she have them come with her to look for the campsite? Was she supposed to make those decisions? For the first time that day, she was unsure and afraid. Truly afraid. What if she found her sister's body today? What if they never found them at all?

"We'll check out the prison and see what we have to work with," Felix offered quickly. He could tell that she was afraid. She could see it reflected in his eyes. She had taken him on hundreds of dives, and he had never once been afraid because neither had she—not really, not like this.

Val nodded stiffly and then shuffled away with Calvin. They walked side by side for a few minutes before he picked a direction and she picked hers, each taking a broad circle around the prison to search for any signs of the land team.

Val felt numb, trudging through long grass and avoiding thorny bushes. Her heart beat wildly in her chest, her eyes skimming her surroundings. Any second now, she imagined that she would come across destroyed tents and ravaged sleeping bags. She imagined Julie's eyes wide and mouth open in that silent scream. What if the jungle life had already taken her body? What if it hadn't? Would she be able to leave Julie the way she'd left Oliver?

She hugged the camera to her chest so hard that the lens cover pressed a circular bruise under her breast. She had forgotten she was carrying it. She hadn't thought of it since she saw Megan's corpse.

Her steps came to an abrupt stop, and for the first time in what felt like—and might have been—hours, she stood completely still. Val blinked, unseeing for long seconds before she realized she was staring straight ahead at a tree. A thick, old tree with a veiny trunk and one fresh chunk gouged out of its side. Her jaw trembled, and she ran those last yards to it, reaching out to touch the scar. Her fingers stayed with the bark when she walked around it, another blaze on the other side and a wide, smooth patch of flattened grass in the shapes of three narrow tents.

Val's legs gave out, and she didn't resist the pull of gravity. She sat there in the place of one of those now-gone tents and cried. She cried until she couldn't breathe, dragging in ragged breaths and letting them out in heaving exhales. Her body doubled forward, one hand leaving the camera to press into the ground, tears sliding off her cheeks and nose to dab the flattened blades of green. She cried so long and so hard that her head hurt and her eyes ached in their sockets, and when she sat upright again, she found daylight fading, drawing them closer and closer to night.

She sat on her heels and stared off into the trees.

A small deer, miniature almost, appeared from a bush and stopped to stare back at her. It had short, pointy horns and dark brown fur. It blinked with big eyes, and she could only stare back, a distant part of her remembering the jaguar dead on the stream with blood seeping from its eyes and deer tracks on its back. The tiny creature bounded away and disappeared almost as easily as it had appeared, leaving her alone again with the sudden, horrible realization that in a jungle she was never alone.

Chapter 12

The sun vanished into the trees, and when Val returned to the front of the old prison, an orange light glowed from inside. It was alive, moving and swaying and sending shadows dancing between the dirt-coated walls. Val followed Felix and Poppy's voices inside, wedging past the tree in the doorway.

Empty cells lined both sides of the hallway, dark without windows. A few of the barred doors were still locked, though many were missing or off their hinges.

Val made her way straight toward the fire built in the hallway beneath a large cavity in the ceiling. Felix and Poppy stopped talking when they saw her, the flames darkening their expressions with sinister shadows. "We found a flint!" Poppy explained the fire with a rush of relief in her voice. She had always been the kind of person to stay positive, so this achievement had probably meant a great deal to her.

"There's not much else here," Felix added, a little more resigned. His tired voice hung heavy in the muggy air. "There were a few old machetes, but they're too rusted to be useful." He walked around Poppy to point at a wall near the fire, and Val came closer to see. The flames rose off a bed of branches and mulch with what looked to be old mattresses beneath. The fire occupied a portion of the floor and climbed up the wall to reach for the empty sky above with smoke fingers. It churned out more embers than flames.

Felix tapped the wall, and it sounded like paper. She looked up at it, squinting at first to see the faded lines in the firelight. A large map of the island with "Isla de los Perdidos" scrawled across the top had been pinned to the wall with thick nails. A black circle marked where the prison stood, and blue lines formed the rivers and streams.

Calvin came in with an armful of branches. Either he'd already been back, or he'd seen the smoke on his way. He stood beside them and looked at the map. "Did you find the campsite?"

Val nodded and tapped a spot on the map on the north side of the prison. "It's here. And I found their trail. We can set out at dawn," she said, untying her sweatshirt from her waist and giving it another good shake before pulling it on. "It looks like we should pass a few more streams," Val said, nudging her chin toward the map. "We can stop to rest and drink when we do."

Poppy nodded and then leaned in a little closer to whisper. "We might have to carry Maeko," she said carefully. "She isn't handling things well."

Calvin groaned and looked around. "Where are they?"

Felix nudged his chin toward one of the nearest doors. "It's an office. She's stopped talking completely. We were hoping she might calm down if she couldn't see the cells or the jungle, but she hasn't said anything. She just keeps shaking her head and staring at the floor."

Val sighed and nodded. "She's in shock. All right. We'll see if we can get her to walk in the morning."

Calvin clicked his teeth angrily and started toward the office. Val caught his wrist before he got far. He turned on her, and she hoped that somewhere in the exhaustion of her face he could see a little plea. "Don't talk to her. Just let her rest and calm down, okay?"

He looked like he might argue before finally letting out a breath and nodding sharply.

She let go of his wrist and watched him walk through the open door into the office. "Are you asleep?" he asked, voice quiet, and she heard the mumbled reply of a still-awake Lochner.

Val looked down at the camera in her hands; she hadn't even tried turning it on yet.

"Should we go outside?" Felix asked, suddenly beside her.

If there was anything on the camera, it might not be something they wanted everyone to see.

Val nodded stiffly, and Felix turned to Poppy to ask her to keep an eye on the fire. He promised to be back soon.

On their way down that long, dark hall, Val turned on the camera. It came to life with a buzz of sound and little red and green lights. She opened the viewfinder out to the side, and the screen lit up with that soft LED glow. A selection of files lined up in neat squares of screen caps. "The last one was this morning," Val whispered and came to a stop near that broken wall at the back of the prison.

Felix's chest pushed against her shoulder when he leaned over to see the screen.

She clicked play on that last file, and it jumped to life. A blur of greens and running legs. They could hear Megan panting as she sprinted, crying whenever she gathered enough breath. There was a rustling growing louder and louder until something hit her from behind. She let out a scream that turned into a sob. The camera smacked against the grassy ground when she fell, and they saw her hands clawing at vegetation and dirt. The camera swung against her chest, the strap around the back of her neck. They couldn't even be sure if she knew it was on.

"Leave me alone!" she screamed, and the speakers crackled.

Megan got to her feet again, and the camera swung violently when she ran. Between gut-wrenching sobs, she continued to beg to be left alone. The bright morning sun flared in the lens. Her footfalls slowed, and the blurry image settled when she finally came to a stop. She panted heavily, and they saw her hands press to her knees when she bent forward, gasping for air. "Please," she begged, crying so hard that she hiccupped. She turned around, and they saw a half circle of the forest before she stopped again.

Felix swore in a low whisper, and Val sucked at air, leaning closer to the camera. Someone stood in front of Megan, but even though it was day and the camera focused clearly, the person was nothing by black streaks, like shadows smeared across the lens. When it walked toward her, the camera crackled, as though those moving smudges were alive and hissing violently against the constraints of the footage. It rushed at her in those last few yards, swallowing up the space between them too quickly, and Megan let out a high scream just before it hit her.

They watched through the lens as the world moved, thrown high before landing violently. Branches cracked and leaves fell all around, but neither Megan nor the camera returned to the ground. For minutes that felt impossibly long, they waited, seeing nothing but her knees and the jungle treetops.

She didn't make any sounds or move again. They watched until the branches started moving and the howler monkeys came. In the carnage that filled the next few minutes, the camera strap broke and fell from her neck, the image cutting out.

Val and Felix stood in the dark corner of the prison and stared at the blank screen.

"What was that?" Felix broke the silence with a breathy whisper.

Val shook her head and clicked the button to take them back to the menu. She opened the second to last file from earlier that morning. It was just walking footage around dawn. Julie talked about birds and pointed them out to Henry. They looked well enough, but Val could hear the stress in Julie's voice. She wasn't excited or happy like she usually was on these trips. Water ran in the background, and then Henry asked, "What's that?" and the camera dropped to stare at the ground before turning off again.

Val went back another file, this one timestamped from last night. The image came to life in a tent to the sound of heavy rain. It turned and focused on Megan's face. She struggled to hold the camera steady, eyes puffy from crying. "There's something wrong with this place," she whispered. Even over the storm, people could be heard arguing in another tent nearby. It sounded like Julie and Zach, but Val had never heard them shout at each other before. She'd actually never heard Zach shout at anyone before.

Megan swallowed hard, eyes glassy with tears. "I think something's been following us," she admitted, the camera wobbling in one hand when she let go with the other to scrub her fingers against her cheeks and catch those freshly fallen tears. "E-everyone is acting weird," she whispered, unable to catch her tears fast enough. She looked around, made more anxious by the end of that shouting match outside her tent. "I think whatever was following us..." she said hurriedly, swallowing hard. "I think it caught up."

The sound of her tents zipper being drawn down brought a small scream up from her throat, and the camera turned off.

"Maybe she was losing her mind," Felix whispered. "She could have had a breakdown and run off."

Val nodded, going through older footage but finding only the usual nature shots. "Then how do you explain what attacked her?" she whispered back.

"Camera malfunction?" Felix didn't sound convinced, but it felt better to pretend than to admit something horrific was stalking the forest and killing people. "It could have been a boar."

"It wasn't shaped like a boar," Val muttered grimly.

She went through all of the footage, fast-forwarding through most of it. They had gone all the way back to the first day when Felix suddenly told Val to stop and rewind. She went back a dozen frames and then pressed play.

"Careful," Julie's voice whispered, tinged with a smile that anyone would be able to hear. Megan zoomed in, the camera focusing beautifully on the jungle floor with a large tree in focus. "We might not have noticed the jaguar at all if we hadn't been looking at the macaws," Julie explained to the camera. The birds fluttered in the branches of the nearby trees but not in the one centered in the frame.

Val touched the screen in front of her, rubbing her finger against it and the spot on the branch where the colors bent and smeared, turning scratchy.

"It has to be some kind of camera malfunction," Felix said, more determined to find a way for it to be true now. It wasn't the same figure they saw in the last footage of Megan, but it was the same sort of distorted picture.

"This is about where we were when we saw the dead jaguar," Val muttered.

The voices of Megan and Julie started to argue on the recording when Megan couldn't get the picture of the big cat. Julie took the camera from her but couldn't do any better. Eventually, it turned off.

There were only two more files before they were back to the Charlene doing interviews. There was nothing else of interest. Val closed the viewfinder and turned off the camera. She looked up and found herself gazing out past that broken prison wall at the dark jungle. Greens so deep they turned black, shifting with branches and leaves and so much more. Val held her breath until it burned in her chest. The jungle stared back.

"What do we tell the others?" Felix whispered.

"Nothing. We can't tell them what we don't know, and we still have to keep moving."

Felix nodded slowly, and she realized that he was staring out into the trees as well. He pulled at her waist to tug her back into the prison shadows. "We should get some rest then," he said quietly, resigned and maybe trying not to think more about what they couldn't be certain of. Camera malfunction was the best answer they had. It was the safest and most sensible. It was the only explanation they had that wasn't nightmarish.

Poppy stood in the firelight, her back to the wall near the office door. She looked up when they returned but didn't ask where they'd been or what was on the camera Val hugged tightly to her chest. Felix dragged a few more branches to the fire, tossing them on. It wasn't really cold enough to need it, but it kept some of the bugs and most of the shadows away. Val sunk down to sit with her back to the wall, and Poppy joined her.

The jungle only got louder at night. Things were waking up to hunt out the ones now sleeping. Bats fluttered through the prison on floppy wings, landing haphazardly against walls and corners. They crawled across the floors like rats, trying to sneak up on them while they slept. She'd been bitten by blood bats before. It wasn't all that noticeable: a sharp cut with expert teeth, and then that eager tongue licking at the wound to drink all it could. Val kicked her leg out to shove one of the little pests away. It screeched angrily and hopped back into the air. They weren't all that dangerous, but she wasn't interested in offering up a meal.

"So," Poppy whispered when she couldn't fall asleep. "What went wrong here that they had to close the prison down?"

Val turned her head to look at Poppy. The younger woman looked tired, in her body and in her soul, and Val imagined for a moment that they were mirrors of one another. They looked nothing alike in most ways, but at that moment, in all ways that mattered, they were identical. Both afraid but pretending not to be. Both tired beyond belief but unable to sleep. Both lost and grappling at the last tendrils of hope.

Turning her head forward again, Val stared at the embers of the fire across from them. Large bugs flew to the flames every so often, unable to resist, and crackled violently when they burned.

"Julie said it was a bunch of ghost stories," she explained, warning in case Poppy wanted to change her mind about hearing them.

The young woman heaved out a laugh before sucking it back into her chest, not wanting to wake the others just around the corner in the office. Felix might have been asleep, too, leaning against the wall on the other side of Poppy. "Well, having spent a few hours here, I couldn't imagine anything less than a ghost story would come out of this place."

Val smiled a little. "Supposedly, there's a village of houses here somewhere on the island, built by an early settlement attempt. The villagers all died before they could bring up a single crop, and that was the beginning of the ghost stories. Soldiers came to investigate the deaths but were never seen again. Decades later, a new government on the mainland tried to use the preexisting village to house their sick during the plague. They pretty much just dumped the infected in rowboats with some supplies and sent them to shore."

"They used this island for quarantine?" Poppy whispered, her face and shoulders tensed with new alarm.

"It was a long time ago. And no one survived. The people on the mainland made up ghost stories for that, too, saying that the island was cursed and something terrible lived here, but it's more likely they just died from their illnesses and exposure." She reassured as best she could, remembering that strange figure on the camera and Megan's face upside down in the tree. Val tucked her arms around herself. "The old quarantine inspired the mainland government to build this prison later on. They thought it would be a great way to put criminals someplace out of the way."

Poppy nodded, eyes closing, finally giving in to exhaustion. "So, what went wrong?"

"Everything," Val answered quietly.

Poppy opened her eyes. "What?"

"They struggled with construction. Men would get inexplicably sick. The animals attacked them frequently. It took twice as long as expected just to build the prison, and they had to send in more and more supplies. Supposedly, a few went mad during the construction and attacked the others, becoming some of the first inmates of the prison they'd helped build." Val watched another bat hop along the shadows just outside the light of the fire. It dropped belly down and started crawling, using those little fingers and toes to propel itself silently closer and closer to her leg. "They only sent two rowboats of inmates to the island. When the soldiers came back months later with supplies as planned, none of the prison guards came to the beach to meet them. Forced to go inland to the prison themselves, the four soldiers found no one here."

Poppy squirmed, chewing her lip. "No one?"

"Not a single body," she confirmed before shrugging and kicking the bat away from her just as it was so close to victory. It rolled on the dirty floor and screamed angrily, coming at her a second time before taking the hint her shoe was offering and flying away. "Only two of the soldiers made it back to the beach where, according to the story, one shot the other and then swam for the ship to give his report. He said the island was a place of madness and that God did not want them there. He said the devil was on this island."

Poppy pushed her back tighter to the wall, tipping her chin up a little. "I don't believe in the devil," she said too quietly.

Val closed her eyes and tried to settle into her spot against old bricks, still harboring delusions of an hour or two of sleep before dawn. "It's just a name. What you call something else, he might have called the devil. The same terror, just different names."

Poppy let out a sigh. "Do you believe in the devil?"

Val wasn't sure how to answer. She only knew nature. The nature of the ocean. The nature of the land. The nature of people. Did she believe in the devil or something wicked and inhuman called by that name in this place? She opened her eyes to look at the fire again. It had grown low and crackled, little flakes of red cooling quickly to ash and drifted away. "I believe something is wrong on this island," she admitted. "And I'm going to do everything I can to get us off of it."

Poppy was quiet for a long time. So long that Val thought she'd finally fallen asleep. And then she whispered, so low that if she weren't sitting right next to her, she would never have heard it. "No one from the village made it off. No one from the quarantine went home. No one from the prison was found. What if no one gets to leave the island, Val?"

"They're stories," she whispered back. "Exaggerations to scare people." She shifted to nudge her shoulder into Poppy's. "And at least one guy made it off in one of those stories, right?"

Poppy let out a laugh of nerves and embarrassment. She nodded once before closing her eyes and wiggling against the wall, trying to find sleep.

Val gave up on trying. She sat there in the quiet and watched the shadows, listening to the sounds of the jungle just outside those crumbling walls.

Just about everyone that had ever been thrown at this place vanished. They were all stories she hadn't given a second thought to when Julie first told her about them. She'd never put stock in ghost stories before. She'd never even given them enough thought to consider herself a non-believer. She simply never needed to contemplate the possibility before. Now, sitting in the dark on Isla de los Perdidos, Val wondered very seriously if there wasn't something horrible there with them. Something that had been there longer than the collapsing prison walls, longer than the trees, maybe even longer than the sand.

Chapter 13

Morning came, but darkness clung to the sky in the form of thick clouds. They left the prison in near silence, trudging through the abandoned campsite to find the trail again and march toward what they could only hope was rescue from this place. Their stomachs growled, calling out to one another, or maybe to the birds in the trees and the snakes in the grass.

They didn't talk on their way from the prison to the creek, shoes scuffing to a stop on the narrow bank. It wasn't until they'd filled their bellies with water that anyone felt like breaking the silence, moods a fraction lighter.

Felix spoke first. "We shouldn't stay here long."

Val nodded. "If we pick up the pace, we can reach the land team's second campsite by midday and then push on to the third." She didn't want to say aloud that they might get lucky and the team would still be there. She thought it, clutched at it in her heart, but she wouldn't say it. She was too afraid of the disappointment that would hit her tonight if they reached that third sight and find they were still another day behind the land team.

"How are we supposed to catch up with them if they're still moving?" Maeko's voice strained in panic and frustration.

Val ignored the way it made her skin tight. They were all frustrated and afraid, so why did Maeko get to be the one freaking out? "The land team is carrying more equipment, and they're moving slowly to film. They're not trying to get anywhere fast, so we should catch up with them, if not today, then tomorrow at the latest."

Poppy nodded before heading upstream a little. She wasn't as interested in sitting still as the others. Her nerves needed movement, and Val could sympathize.

"But what about Megan?" Lochner interjected, beard shining with beads of water. "The land team might not know she's dead, but they have to know she's missing. Would they really still be moving forward?"

Val almost cringed. Those were the questions she'd been asking herself all night. "They would come back the same way, and we haven't seen them or any signs of them."

"Maybe they think she went back to shore?" Felix offered.

"Or maybe they've tried contacting the ship and are bunkered down at one of the campsites," Calvin suggested, hopeful despite his sour expression this morning.

He seemed to have taken on Maeko duty this morning, glaring at the woman as though willing her out of her shock. Val hoped he wouldn't succeed. Right now, Maeko was dazed and sour, but at least she was walking. If they could keep her moving, and hopefully moving quickly, they might just catch up to Julie, Zach, and Henry today.

Felix stood from where he'd crouched at the stream, stretching his back before looking around. His expression fell hard, head whipping from one side to the other. "Where's

Poppy?"

Val looked up the river in the direction the other woman had gone. "Poppy!" she called, waiting half a second without response before starting up the hill. She climbed a thick nest of roots at the top, pushing herself over and stumbling a few steps to get her balance. The stream rolled by, bouncing off rocks and roots. It was thin but clear, and there wasn't much more they could ask for.

"Val?" Felix called up after her.

"I see her," she called back, a verbal wave-off, and started walking toward Poppy. The other woman stood just upstream with her back to her.

"What are you doing?" Val asked just as she came up behind her. Her shoes dug into the wet ground when she stopped, staring over Poppy's shoulder at the dam. It wasn't much, but it wasn't natural—waist high and made of shoes. A pile of shoes for bricks and the rare bit of canvas for mortar. They looked old, like antiques. Boots as well as slippers. Adult sized as well as child. At least a hundred pairs of shoes piled up to form a dam across the stream.

Val walked around it to the other side. The water upstream was at least waist deep and pooled against the barrier, seeping through the cracks to trickle out in a thin creek. She looked back at Poppy to see quiet tears rolling down those cheeks. "No one leaves the island," she whispered, and Val felt sick.

She caught Poppy's elbow and turned her away from the eerie structure, nudging her back toward the others in a slow march.

"What is it?" Poppy whispered, not looking back.

Val moved close beside her. "I don't know. Something left over from past settlements, maybe."

Poppy didn't nod, but she didn't say anything else

either.

They returned to the others just as Calvin got impatient. He wanted to press on. The new day brought with it a new desperation to find the others on the island and the emergency beacon they carried. Poppy didn't say anything about the shoes, and Val felt a wave of relief. It was creepy, but it wasn't something they needed to talk about, and there was no point in adding more fear to the hearts of their traveling party.

They walked fast, with no attempts at light conversation today. The morning melted away, and they only stopped to take bathroom breaks. The water moved through them too quickly, leaving everyone empty, hungry, thirsty, and tired by midday.

"We're almost there," Val urged them, eyes always searching ahead, not just for the next marked tree in the trail, but for flattened grass and signs of the second campsite. She almost missed her step when she saw a bright yellow tent sticking out from the greens of the trees and bushes ahead. Her breath rushed out of her, launching into a sprint.

Calvin called after her, surprised, but soon their hurried steps followed.

"Julie!" Val shouted, pushing a branch out of her way and bursting into the campsite. All hope drained from her chest, sinking right down to pool in her gut. Everything was there. Three tents the size of sleeping bags, backpacks, and camera equipment. Water bottles, clothing, packets of food—everything was there, but no one was.

She turned full circle. The radio sat in the grass in pieces. Smashed. Lochner knelt beside it, immediately setting to work trying to get it to turn on.

Calvin grabbed the bags and started emptying them

out with no care for the belongings inside. The only thing he was interested in finding was the emergency beacon. He cursed loudly at every failed search.

Maeko touched a tent absently, and Poppy kept a wary eye on her while Felix walked a full circle around the camp.

"Julie!" Val screamed again.

"It's not here!" Calvin shouted angrily, throwing the last bag he'd pulled from one of the tents. He clawed fingers through his sweaty hair and squeezed his eyes shut.

"One of them has to have it then, right?" Poppy said, reasonable even now. They had to be close. They'd reached the campsite, and from the looks of it, it was the last one. They hadn't packed up any of their things, tents still up and bags open. They hadn't moved on to another spot after the second night. Had they slept here last night? Were they out in the jungle looking for Megan? Or were they in the trees, dead, like Megan?

"Julie!" Val screamed, turning in another direction, staring out into the endless green and waiting for an echo that never came.

"There's blood over here," Felix said, voice heavy. Calvin and Poppy moved closer to see the matted grass and the thick, red puddle. It looked black on the ground but red on his fingers when he touched it.

"What the fuck happened here?" Poppy demanded.

"Maybe those monkeys attacked them?" Calvin said quietly, sounding skeptical himself.

Val heard a branch snap, and her body whirled to the right. She found only tents and jungle and Maeko standing very still. She had turned her head to look, too. Val took two steps closer, and Maeko reached out to point toward a tall bush against the side of a tree.

Val walked past her, trusting her to stay quiet.

The others continued to argue, voices growing loud enough to camouflage her steps as she neared that bush. Its branches shuddered, and her heart beat wildly. She could see the toes of hiking boots at the base of the greenery and dirty hands hugging knees. Sucking in a deep breath, she reached out and grabbed a handful of those long branches. She swept the body of the plant aside and leaned around to see, tense and ready for anything after what she'd already seen on this island.

Henry let out a scream, jerking in his hiding place to thump his head against the trunk of the tree. His hands came up, arms out and guarding his tear-streaked face. He shook his head, choking out a trail of sobs that sounded as though they'd been locked in his throat for hours. "It's not me! It's not me!" he shouted frantically.

Felix hurried over, whatever frustrated nerves they'd been shouting out had come to a sudden halt when they heard the new voice. He came around Val, took in the sight of Henry, and immediately softened. He crouched down and put a hand on Henry's shoulder, shushing him.

"Where's Julie?" Val demanded. It came out harsh, but it was the only question she could think of.

Felix squeezed Henry's shoulder, rocking the younger man gently where he sat. Henry's arms collapsed to his sides, chest heaving to drag in ragged breaths.

"What happened?" Felix asked in a softer voice.

Henry continued to cry, pushing his forehead against his knees. "It's one of them. It's not me," he repeated.

"What's not you?" Poppy asked, standing behind Val.

Henry shook his head, looking up at her. "Julie says it's Zach, but Zach says it's Julie." He scrubbed his dirty hands against his cheeks to try to rub away his tears. "She broke the radio!" he blurted out, and then shook his head and shushed himself. "She said Zach would use it to get off the island, but there is no getting off the island."

Felix rubbed Henry's shoulder, nodding patiently while Val bit her lip to keep from shouting. She twisted away from them, walking a tight circle to get control of herself. She wanted to shake the frightened man for answers.

"What happened?" Felix asked again, voice quiet and calm.

Henry heaved breaths that came so erratically he sounded like he might suffocate. "Julie attacked Zach, and I hid," he confessed.

Val froze, resisting the urge to look back at the patch of blood on the grass in the campsite. "She attacked him?"

He nodded. "With a knife. I hid. I heard them shouting and fighting. One chased the other into the woods, I heard it, but I...I couldn't look," he choked out the words, scrubbing at his eyes with the backs of dirty hands. "It's not me. It's not me."

They couldn't get much more out of him.

It took Felix twenty minutes just to get Henry up and move him back into the campsite. Val hoped he managed to coax a few more answers out of Henry before he finally curled up in one of those tents, rocking himself to sleep. "One of them has to have the beacon," Calvin decided after he and Poppy circled the campsite, searching for the rescue device. It wasn't very big, but it would have a flashing red light on it that should, ideally, make it easier to find.

Val nodded from where she sat. Lochner gave up on the radio and took to organizing the available supplies and food. He opened a bag of jerky and started passing it around, followed by a jug of water. Val tried not to think about if it had come from the stream beside the dam of shoes. She drank down a large gulp.

"We should stay here then," she decided. "In case Julie or Zach comes back." Her gaze cut to the bloody spot in the grass on the other side of the campsite. At least one of them was injured, possibly worse if that fight had continued out in the jungle.

Val struggled to believe Henry. Julie had never physically attacked anyone before, and she hadn't been in a scuffle since middle school, which was almost too pathetic of a fight to even count. And Zach wouldn't even kill bugs, always more of a catch-and-release sort of person.

"What if they don't come back?" Calvin asked, sitting down across from her and beside Lochner.

"We'll go looking for them," she decided for them all. Val hadn't liked the responsibility of leading the way yesterday, but now she couldn't imagine giving it to anyone else.

"Are you kidding?" Maeko finally spoke, voice raw. She'd been sitting in the mouth of one of those little tents since they found Henry. "We have to get out of here."

"We need the beacon for that."

"Fuck the beacon," Maeko snapped. "We go back to the beach. We make a fire or something to signal for help, and we get off this island."

"The chance of anyone seeing it and coming out are slim," Felix reminded her, swallowing the jerky he'd been chewing. "If we can find the beacon, we can at least send out a rescue signal."

Maeko grabbed desperately for another option. "What about when we don't show up to resupply at the docks. They'll realize something happened to us and send someone."

"The mainlanders expected us to die," Calvin pointed out grimly. "They think this place is haunted or cursed or whatever. You saw their faces when we said where we were going."

Maeko grew terribly still again, and Val could almost see the woman sinking back into herself until those dark eyes met hers, flaring to life anew. "You're going to kill us."

Everyone looked up. They stopped chewing or drinking and stared in surprise at Maeko, but Maeko only looked at Val. "You'd drag us out into the jungle to look for her even if we had the beacon. I bet if you'd found it, you would have hidden it..."

Felix cursed in Spanish and shook his head, looking away.

Val stared back at Maeko. "Her? You mean Julie. You mean my sister." She leaned forward, closer to Maeko. "If I had the beacon, I would have pushed the button and sent your whining ass back to the beach. But you're right, I wouldn't leave without my sister. I would still be here, but I wouldn't keep you." She clicked her teeth angrily. "Can you think of any reason I would keep you, Maeko? What use have you been to me?"

Maeko hissed angrily but finally turned and crawled into the tent behind her. She pulled the zipper down, and Val suspected it was as close to a slammed door as they were going to get.

The sun sank behind the trees, deeper and deeper out of sight until the last of the colors in the sky went with it. They were fast full on jerky and protein bars.

"Did Henry say anything about Megan?" Lochner asked quietly.

Felix nodded grimly. "He said she ran off yesterday morning. They thought she'd gone mad. I guess she'd been rambling about her camera and someone following them." He took another drink of water before passing it to Calvin.

"She attacked Julie in the morning when they were getting ready to pack up the second campsite. Zach pulled her off of Julie, but he couldn't keep hold of Megan, and she took off. He said they looked for her all morning and then Julie got so pissed she wanted to pack up and move on like they'd planned."

Calvin looked surprised. "She wanted to leave her behind?"

Felix shrugged uncomfortably. "I guess she thought Megan knew their travel plan so she could catch up on her own? I don't know. Julie and Zach ended up arguing and, well, here we are."

Calvin shook his head and closed his eyes. "What the hell is wrong with this place?" he whispered before leaning against Lochner's side.

Val understood what he meant. It didn't sound right. Julie wouldn't have moved on and left Megan behind. And they wouldn't have attacked each other and disappeared into the jungle. Val looked at Felix and saw the same unease reflected in his eyes. Were they really going to take Henry's word? She wanted to say it aloud but didn't need to; she could feel it in the air between them. They couldn't be sure what had happened until they found Julie and Zach.

Just before the sun went down completely, they found the fourth tent in the pile of clothing that had come from Megan's pack. Calvin set it up. Poppy agreed to share a tent with Maeko while Val and Felix squeezed into one and Lochner and Calvin into the last. They let Henry keep his own to himself, as no one was eager to crawl in and wake the hysterical cameraman.

It was a tight fit, two people in one little tent. Mashed up against Felix's side, Val imagined it was an even tighter squeeze for Calvin and Lochner.

She lay her head against Felix's chest, using him for a pillow and draping one leg over his. It wasn't unlike how they used to sleep. They'd always been snugglers. She was surprised Felix didn't complain or shift her a little off of him in this muggy heat though. He used to say that she was a thousand degrees, his own heater in the winter. But he didn't push her away or seek out some cooler air. His arm squeezed her waist, and his other hand touched the back of her neck, as though he worried she might move away. She smiled a little against his shirt because, in this tent, there was nowhere to go.

The jungle hummed with life outside, and every so often bugs smacked against the thin tent, some bouncing off and others staying to scuttle about the surface. Zipped up inside that thin nylon was the first time she actually felt like she could breathe since they crawled ashore. She was contained and, for a moment, the jungle was someplace else.

"My ring was on the boat," Val whispered just as it occurred to her, the smallest pang of loss creeping into her heart.

She felt him smiling. It was in his fingertips against her skin and his chest beneath her ear. It was in the sticky air of the tent all around her.

"I knew you still had it," he replied in gentle triumph.

"Well, we are married," Val said quietly, closing her eyes.

He squeezed her a little tighter for her confession. "Oh, now I'm worried. You haven't admitted that in years."

She opened her eyes again in the dark and thought of things she could say. It was true. She hadn't admitted it. She'd been punishing him for not listening to her, for not following her, for not giving in. And she'd been punishing herself for all the same reasons. She let out a little sigh because they were sometimes too much alike.

"Julie might be dead," Val whispered, her voice cracking a little on that last word. He held her tighter but didn't interrupt. "Whatever happened, I think Henry and Megan were right. I think there's something on this island." She kept her voice quiet, knowing the nylon of their tent was no privacy at all. "But I'm going to get us off this island," Val promised. "I'm yours and your mine, and I'm going to get you off this island."

He turned his head into her hair and kissed her forehead, leaving his lips there. "I love you, too, *sirenita.*"

Val sighed and closed her eyes. It was easier to sleep in the tent than it had been in the prison or on the beach. Those thin walls of fabric gave the illusion of safety. Zippers might as well have been steel doors with deadbolts. But whatever deep sleep she'd felt soon dwindled into disturbing dreams. Piles of bodies. Julie and Zach with blood rolling down their faces from their eyes and noses, lying naked in a heap. Clear water ran over them, coming from nowhere but impossibly loud, rolling along their limbs and between the creases of their bodies pressed together.

Val stood above them. Over all of them. And looked down, first at the stream below, running in a delicate trickle down the rocks, and then in the other direction, at the ocean. When she turned to the jungle again, that figure was there, standing in the trees. It was scratchy and distorted, just like on the camera, and no matter how she blinked, she couldn't see it clearly.

It came at her. Grabbed her. Leaned in close and whispered in her ear, *"You're not you."*

Chapter 14

Val woke in the tent, in the dark. She propped herself up on her elbows, as high as she could without pushing her head against the slanted roof. The legs of a beetle scraped against the nylon near her ear. She turned her head toward it just as it flew off, wings buzzing and disappearing into the night. Silence never came. Real silence didn't seem to exist on Isla de los Perdidos.

She heard sobbing, muffled but present. She listened for a few more minutes to that incoherent mumbling, too soft and far away to even begin to make out.

Val rolled onto her stomach and grabbed the flashlight. She turned it on and wiggled forward to grab at the zipper of the tent and tug it open.

Felix groaned when he stirred, hands seeking out her hips. His eyes opened to squint up at her and the light when some part of his sleeping brain registered her retreat. "Val?" Her mumbled name held a dozen questions.

"I'm gonna check on Henry. Go back to sleep," she whispered, giving one of his hands a squeeze before crawling out of the tent and zipping it back up. She stood and stretched, suddenly alone in the dark. The flashlight should have been a comfort, giving her sight in the pitch black, but it only made her feel like a lighthouse in the sea. She could see little, and all could see her.

Henry's tent was only three big steps from hers. She squatted down. "Henry." She whispered his name, shining the light through the blue nylon of his tent. He stopped his mumbling and twisted toward her light. He sniffled, lying still. She tugged down the zipper enough to have the mouth of his tent flop open part way so she could see his tear-wet face and he could see her. "You all right?"

He sniffled again, dragging in a big breath and nodding. It was almost laughable because it was so obviously a lie. He wasn't all right. He was probably in the middle of a nervous breakdown. "Can...can we leave the island tomorrow?" Henry begged, and she felt immediately uncomfortable. She didn't like the way it sounded, like the decision was hers and he was so desperately hoping that she would finally let them go home.

She was about to answer when his face twisted in terror and his body tensed, straining back and away from her. Val felt her spine tighten when she watched his frightened gaze fix on something behind her. She turned, still crouched to look up and back, lifting the flashlight. There was no stretch of jungle leading into the dark or the bright yellow tent she'd left Felix in. The light soaked into Julie's face, the woman standing right behind her. Val sucked in a surprised breath and almost fell back into Henry's tent.

Julie stood there, so close but without a sound. Little shudders shook her frame, and her hair was just as wet and filthy as the rest of her. Mud and blood caked her clothes and skin.

Val jumped to her feet, dropping the flashlight to grab onto her sister's arms. She needed to feel her to believe she was real. "Holy shit." She let out that breath she'd sucked in, squeezing the arms she'd grabbed. Julie was solid and sticky with sweat. "Are you okay?" Val asked automatically, even though she struggled to care if her sister was banged up or a total wreck. She was alive and right there in the camp.

Val pulled her in and hugged her tight, touching her back and her shoulders, a part of her still desperate to make sure it wasn't a dream. "Where the hell have you been? What happened?" She continued to ask questions when she didn't get an answer, suddenly needing to hear her sister's voice.

Julie mumbled a reply into her hair, and Val pulled back, holding her sister by the shoulders now. "What?" she asked softly, and watched in surprise as her sister's expression crumbled. She started to cry, not the way she had as a child, with the full force of her vocal cords and all the tears her body could produce, or even the way she had as an adult, with sensible, gentle hiccups. Julie trembled and heaved breath, swallowing back broken sobs while thick tears gleamed in her eyes.

She shook her head, blood crusted to the side of her neck and cheek. "You're not you," Julie said again, and before Val could scrunch her face and ask what she meant, her sister lunged at her.

Julie tackled her to the ground in front of Henry's tent. The fall pushed the air up from Val's lungs just before those cold, muddy fingers wrapped around her throat and clamped down. She grabbed at Julie's wrists and tried to pull them off, but the grip on her neck only tightened. Val kicked at the grass to try to roll them over, but

Julie put her knees firmly to the ground, the toes of her boots digging in.

Val thought she heard howling, some distant part of her mind wondering if there were wolves on this damned island, too, before quickly realizing that Henry had begun to scream.

Val reached up, mouth gasping for air she couldn't suck down, and clawed fingers at her sister's face and neck. She tried to reach her sister's eyes, but Julie leaned her head back to stay out of reach.

Those fingers pressed harder, firm and unrelenting. Val couldn't breathe, not at all, and her head throbbed. She grabbed again at Julie's wrist and pulled, nails cutting into skin. Her other hand balled into a fist and swung, trying to ram knuckles into her sister's side, but she wouldn't be moved.

Just as her vision began to blur, Val saw the shape of a person behind Julie. For one awful moment, she thought it was the figure from the camera, the one that had thrown Megan into that tree, and then Felix came up fully behind Julie and lifted her by the armpits. She didn't let go of Val at first, pulling her by the neck so her shoulders and head lifted up off the ground. Val kicked at the beaten-down grass one last time to turn herself, twisting to break her sisters hold on her neck and landing face-down on the ground. She gulped for air and coughed violently.

Julie screamed like a wild animal, kicking and flailing, but Felix was taller and held her up off the ground. He wrapped an arm around her to pin her arms to her sides, cringing and twisting his head back and to the side to avoid her skull when she tried to crack it back against his face. It wasn't elegant, but he held on and walked her a few big steps away from the tents while she spent her energy fighting.

Val shoved away Calvin's first attempt to help her up, lying on her stomach and coughing, fingers pressing into the grass to try to lift her chest up and suck in deeper breaths. Calvin wasn't put off and grabbed onto her shoulder again, pulling until she sat upright and could take deeper breaths. He held onto her shoulders to keep her up, watching her face to make sure her eyes focused on him.

"You okay?" he asked, and she realized that it wasn't the first time.

Val nodded, her breath wheezing in and out and her hands numb. Her face felt hot and swollen, and her lips throbbed. She turned to look at Julie still in Felix's arms but no longer kicking. She poured her energy into screaming instead, sure to wake anyone who had managed to sleep through Henry's shouting and Val's struggle.

"No one leaves the island!" Julie raged, spittle spraying from her lips and face turning a bright pink in her struggle. "You're not you! You can't leave!"

Val stared back at her through the shadows, not recognizing her at all. "Do we have rope?" she wheezed out, her throat raw and her words tight.

Only Calvin managed to hear her and turned to look up at Lochner. "Get the rope. We'll tie her up so she can't hurt anyone else."

Poppy and Maeko stood just outside their tent, watching. "What's wrong with her?" Poppy whispered.

"She's gone mad," Maeko answered bluntly and then crawled back into the tent.

Between Lochner and Felix, they managed to tie Julie's arms behind her back with a thin black rope, leaving a loop on the end of the excess like the handle of a leash. She calmed eventually, relenting to sit in the dirt when they tied her to the nearest tree.

When Val approached her, Julie just stared, teeth bared and lips cracked.

"Where's Zach?" Val asked quietly, voice still strained. Felix and Calvin stood close by.

"Dead," Julie said flatly. "Dead like you."

Val frowned deeply and then swallowed hard, reaching down to pull Julie to her feet. Felix held her shoulder to keep her steady while Val searched her pockets. Handfuls of mud and rocks came out. When she reached around to pop open one of the extra pockets on her cargo pants, Julie hissed and tried to kick her. Felix held fast to her shoulders, and Val pulled out a smooth piece of plastic about the size of a phone.

She felt a collective exhale between the others when she held that blinking beacon in her palm.

Julie foamed at the mouth and tried to kick off from the tree, straining the rope and her wrists when she tried to reach her retreating sister. "No! You can't leave the island! You can't let them leave!" she shouted, mad, but Val wasn't listening to her. She walked away from the tree and her sister and back to the camp. She wiped the beacon clean with her shirt. It only had that gently flashing light to tell that it was still alive and functioning. She pulled at the lid, popping the top off of that hard, bright yellow, plastic shell to expose the single switch.

They all held their breaths when she flipped it to the other side and waited until that red flashing light turned into a solid green. Val swallowed hard and put the lid back on. She looked up at the others, wondering who should carry it. Finally, she held it out toward Poppy. She was the youngest of them, and somehow it seemed right.

Lochner nodded. "Don't lose it," he said gruffly.

Poppy laughed a little at the idea, but that seemed to settle the matter. She took the beacon from Val and stuffed it deep into her front pocket.

The sun soon rose, and other than Maeko, none of them were going back to bed. They decided to head back to the beach in the morning. Why wait for their rescue to come inland if it would save them from spending a couple more days on Isla de los Perdidos? They'd call out for Zach on the way, but Julie offered little hope that they'd find him. She just kept saying he wasn't himself. She had blood caked between her fingers and nails, and they all knew now who the puddle of red in the grass belonged to.

They set themselves to packing up the supplies they could use into the backpacks. Val distributed the food and water bottles evenly between the four bags, in case they lost one or someone had the misfortune of getting separated from the others. There were two first aid kits and a few ziplock bags she hung onto. In one of the pockets of Megan's bag she'd found a small camera, the kind meant for snapshots and short videos that inevitably took up too much space. There wasn't much on it, just a few selfies and snaps of Julie and Zach from the first day. She considered tossing it before finally shoving it back in and zipping it up. It was light, after all, so it wouldn't be much trouble to carry, and some grim part of her heart worried that her sister would want those last happy pictures when she snapped out of whatever madness or shock had overcome her.

Among the supplies, they'd found a few camping knives. Two foldable and one with a sheath and a built-in flint. There was an exchange of looks when it came to the three knives versus the eight travelers. No one was going to give Julie, Henry, or Maeko a weapon, so that left only five. Val pocketed one of the foldable blades and then held up the larger knife between Calvin and Lochner. Calvin took it first and then handed it to his husband, who attached the sheath to his belt. Poppy shook her head when they looked at her, so Val handed the last weapon to Felix, who put it away just before Maeko unzipped her tent and came out.

She looked around at the four bags and dug out a bottle of water to take the last deep gulp it had to offer.

Poppy set to work taking down their tent and folding it up, earning her a sharp look from the other woman. "What are you doing?" Maeko asked, dropping the empty bottle back into the pack. "Does it matter if we leave this stuff behind? It's not like some park ranger is going to see it and give us a fine," she mumbled. It seemed a night of rest had made her more conversational. Val wasn't sure it was a good thing.

Poppy bunched up the nylon and shoved it into the bag with the empty bottle and some other supplies. "We might need it," she answered, trying not to sound grim. "We found a map and a faster route back, but we might still have to camp a night if the sun goes down before we reach the beach."

"A faster route?" Maeko ground out, glaring at the others like they'd tricked her into a longer route on the way up.

"We're not looking for anyone, and we're not exactly sightseeing, so we can ditch the original trail and cut a straight line for the beach," Poppy explained.

Luckily, Maeko didn't argue about heading back to the beach, and she even offered to carry one of the bags for a while. Val took the second, Lochner the third, and Poppy the fourth, while Calvin led the way and Felix took Julie's leash. There was a promise to trade if the packs got too heavy for anyone, but without the clothing and camera equipment, they weren't all that heavy.

They kept Henry walking near the middle of the group so as to keep a collective eye on him. He hadn't said much, but he'd been particularly squeamish about Julie. He'd insisted on taking Megan's camera with him, mumbling something about how all of his had been destroyed and that this would be her last work.

Val hung back in the traveling party enough to talk to Julie. She prodded her for more answers, but Julie only clicked her teeth angrily and glared. She was practically a stranger. In the growing daylight, Val could see better the different stains on her sister's clothing and skin. Mostly mud, but a lot of blood, too. She could only see a few small cuts and bruises on her sister, nothing to explain all that red.

"Whose blood is that?" Val finally asked, walking beside her with Felix just behind.

Julie looked down at her chest, eyes widening just a fraction when she saw the reddish-brown stains on the side of her tank top and crusted on her shoulder and arm. She swallowed hard and looked away. For a second, Val thought she saw remorse in her sister's eyes. For a moment, they were, once again, her sister's. And then Julie tipped her chin up, and it was gone. "It wasn't him," she muttered stubbornly. Val's stomach knotted, wondering if it was just something she had to tell herself now. Julie loved Zach. She'd been planning a life with him. If she had killed him, she would probably have to convince herself it wasn't him.

"Val," Calvin called from ahead. He brought the whole group to a stop.

Val wove through Maeko, Poppy, Henry, and Lochner

to get to him. She touched his shoulder when she did and stopped at his side. Rather than explaining, Calvin stretched one arm forward and pointed between the trees up ahead.

A man stood there, a shadow inside the shadows of trees, watching them.

Chapter 15

Her heart beat faster, remembering the footage and the creature the camera couldn't see.

The figure took a few hobbled steps closer, out from under that particular tree, and the shadows slipped away from his face. Zach swallowcd hard, one hand pressed tight against the side of his thigh while keeping most of his weight on the other leg. He looked as filthy and as tired as Julie.

"I-is she okay?" he called out, voice trembling.

Julie started shouting again, and Felix let out a string of curses when he had to pick her up to keep her from pulling at that leash.

Val ignored her sister and cut a path over the heavily rooted ground to reach Zach. Calvin and the others followed.

Zach sniffled and shook his head, looking past her shoulder to watch Julie flail against Felix's hold. "I don't know what happened to her," he confessed even before Val closed the gap between them. "She lost it and smashed the radio. She kept saying that I wasn't me and Henry wasn't Henry." His gaze moved to the side to see Henry standing there, now trapped between the two and looking acutely uncomfortable. But Zach let out a sigh of relief to see the cameraman. "H-have you found Megan?" he asked when Val reached him, blocking his view of the others.

"What happened to her?" Val asked instead of answering, voice hard.

He looked surprised by her tone, his eyes large and bloodshot. "Who? Megan? She ran off. Yesterday, I think, just before Julie went nuts and attacked me. I followed her into the jungle but got lost." He looked over her shoulder to try to see Julie again. Felix carried her closer, following the others down that sharp hill to meet with Zach. Julie had calmed a little, still pinned against Felix's side.

Zach shuffled around Val's side, and she noticed that the hand pressed to his thigh was coated red and his pant leg was soaked. She let out a curse and rolled her shoulders to drop her bag, bringing it around to rest on her shoes while she unzipped the front and pulled out a first aid kit.

Calvin, never missing a beat, already found a large rock nearby to use as a chair. He grabbed Zach by the arm and helped him over to it, sitting him down. Val passed Calvin the first aid kit. While he rooted through the supplies available, she pulled the knife from her back pocket, flipped it open, and started cutting open Zach's pant leg.

He let out a shaky breath and thanked Lochner when the former captain handed him a bottle of water. "I'm so glad you guys came to find us. I didn't think my call to the ship went through before she smashed the radio," Zach explained.

Lochner's cheek twitched. "Charlene sank."

Zach's eyes grew, but Julie laughed.

"We have the beacon. We're going to meet the rescue at the beach," Maeko repeated the plan almost like a prayer but with an edge of urgency that told everyone she didn't like standing still for this long. It seemed now that she was finally moving, she didn't want to stop.

Calvin opened a bottle of rubbing alcohol and, without warning, poured it on the wound. Zach didn't notice, still watching Julie. Val watched Zach. His eyes were full of sympathy and worry. She nudged her chin toward his leg, the wound there bubbling up more blood now that the mud had been rinsed away. "What happened?" Val asked, voice still hard and words blunt.

Calvin threaded a needle. Val trusted he'd make quick work of the open flesh. He'd stitched her up twice before when they were out at sea together. Lochner once said that there was no point in going anywhere unless someone on the crew could set bones and stitch cuts. It later became his reason never to go anywhere without his husband. There wasn't an injury on the planet that Calvin balked at.

Zach swallowed and looked up at her. Heavy bags hung under his eyes and mud caked his hair. "She attacked me after the radio and then ran off," he explained again. "I was looking for her and got lost."

Val looked back at Henry. The cameraman shifted nervously, trying not to look back at her for too long. Val folded the knife shut and pocketed it, not noticing the way Maeko stared when she did.

"He's not Zach!" Julie shouted, leaning as close to them as she could with Felix still holding her arms. "He's not him!"

"I'm starting to sense a theme to her madness..." Calvin muttered, tying off the last stitch before bandaging the wound.

"We need to get her to a hospital," Val said firmly, and Calvin hummed mildly in agreement. "Will you be able to walk?" she asked Zach.

He nodded, and Calvin helped him get on his feet.

"All right. We'll keep moving until we hit the next stream," Val decided, and no one disagreed.

Zach shuffled toward Julie, reaching for her in concern. Julie let out another scream and reeled back into Felix. Val pushed herself between the couple and grabbed a fistful of Zach's shirt, pushing him back a step and forcing him to turn in the right direction—away from her sister.

"Move," she ordered.

Zach started walking, one leg struggling but body determined.

Val stayed between him and Julie for the rest of the trek downhill. Lochner fell into line to walk at the man's side ahead of her, in case he staggered or fell, and Poppy picked up her steps to join Calvin at the lead, leaving Maeko and Henry to quietly march along behind them.

Val wasn't sure it was a good idea to put Maeko and Henry together, but she didn't have the energy to think of an excuse to separate the two.

Calvin tried to keep the pace up, but inevitably they were slowed by Zach. Maeko made a few sharp sounds through her clenched teeth, but no one said anything. They weren't going to leave him behind, and no one was offering to carry him.

"He's not him."

Val jumped when Julie whispered close to her ear. She twisted to look back at her sister. Her eyes were wild, but she had stopped pulling at the rope Felix held behind her.

"He's not him, Val," she said again, voice low and eyes darting past her shoulder to look at Zach walking ahead of them.

Val sighed and turned her gaze forward again. "Like how I'm not me? And Henry's not Henry?" She felt tired. Tired of this nonsense. Tired of this island. Tired of being confused and lost and afraid.

"You won't always be you," Julie continued, keeping her voice low. "No one can leave the island."

Val cringed. "Shut up, Jules."

"Zach isn't Zach," Julie said again, sharply pronouncing each word. "You know it, don't you? You know."

Val stared ahead, at Zach's back. He struggled with his leg but tried to keep up with Calvin. His shoulders hitched when he sniffled. His arm came up to rub the back of his hand under his nose. She saw the streak of red on his dirty skin before he rubbed it off on his shirt. They were both a mess. Val made some mental note to make sure Zach, as well as Julie, saw a psychologist as well as a physician when they got back home. Something had happened on this island. Julie had attacked and stabbed her fiancé. Though Val knew that everything pointed to her sister being mad, she still couldn't resist keeping a skeptical eye on Zach. Julie was crazed, but she believed there was something wrong with him.

Poppy let out an excited sound up ahead and rushed off from Calvin to break through the netting of bushes and trees.

"Water," Calvin called back before he too disappeared through the foliage.

Maeko whispered something to Henry just before they followed. Whatever she said, Henry looked paler for it.

Lochner pushed aside a few branches and held them

back while Zach struggled over the roots. Val closed the space between them and took his arm, helping him over. Standing close for that moment, she looked up at him. His eyes flared in surprise before a grateful smile broke across his features. He stumbled over the growth of plants and onto the bank of the creek. It was wider than the others had been but not deeper.

Val expected to see Poppy rolling in it to cool down. She was a kindred spirit, of sorts. They both preferred water to land. But Poppy hadn't lain down in this stream. She hadn't even crouched to refill the water bottle in her bag. She just stood there, with Calvin, staring down the alley cut through the ground foliage by the water.

Henry heaved breaths, on the verge of another meltdown, and Maeko passed them all to stand over the pile clogging the water. It wasn't shoes this time. It was a mound of what originally looked like branches and moss. The closer Val got, the more she realized it wasn't wood. It was another dam, making the water wider on their side of it and narrower on the other, but it was built of bones. Val stood beside Maeko and stared at it. Arms and legs and rib cages were piled together. Like the stream, the dam was wider than it was high. The water struggled to find its way through, sparkling where it moved beneath that top layer of bones.

"Where are the heads?" Maeko asked, voice chilled.

Val stared at it and realized that there were no skulls. The others had joined them, looking at the construction.

"Do you think there are cannibals on this island?" Maeko added, and Henry choked on his sounds.

Val gave the other woman a sharp look, hoping to quiet her.

"Who would do this?" Felix wondered.

"He did it," Julie said, mad as ever and glaring bitterly at Zach.

Zach looked tired for it, turning to his fiancé. "Really? I did this?" he asked, sounding more than a little fed up. "This has to be at least a hundred years old, Jules. It's all bones and leaves and moss. When did I do this?"

She leaned toward him, but Felix caught her arm before she could turn it into a full lunge.

"You think I'm a monster, Jules?" Zach snapped, voice rising with new temper. "Fine. I'm a fucking monster." He stepped up onto the bone dam and the rest of them sucked back a collective breath of disgust when it creaked and strained.

"Get the hell off that!" Calvin snapped, but Zach stared at Julie and took steps across. He stood in the middle, the bones bending under his weight but not giving way. The pile was solid.

"I obviously came here a decade ago, before we met, and built this pile of bones to taunt you, right, Julie?" He marched all the way across and jumped down on the other side. Arms out, he turned around to look back at them, staring at Julie. "Did I kill them, too? Did I do that?" he shouted.

Felix mumbled a curse and walked around the dam to the smaller side of the stream. He pulled Julie across the water with him but didn't bring her closer than a few arm lengths to Zach. "Shut up, man. She's sick, and you're just going to piss her off."

Val and Lochner followed next, putting themselves easily between the couple.

"What are you doing?" Calvin shouted, and Val looked back to see Maeko climbing up on the bone bridge, too.

"I don't want to get my shoes wet again," she complained. "They just dried out." She held her arms out to her sides as she walked, femurs, spines, and ribs creaking under her weight.

Calvin let out a string of curses and grabbed Henry by the arm to pull him across the stream. He made choking, heaving sounds now and hugged Megan's camera tightly to his chest. Poppy followed last, struggling to look away from the pile of human remains even when she was on the other side of it with the rest of them.

Lochner took up helping Zach again just as he began favoring his good leg once more. Val watched him struggle away from the scene to follow Calvin and Henry into the jungle. Maeko followed, and eventually, so did Poppy. Felix lingered, seemingly unwilling to leave without Val.

"Does it mean anything to you?" Felix asked, voice low, the sounds of their traveling party moving away from them.

Val gave the bone bridge one last, hard look, and when she tore her gaze from it and turned toward her husband and the jungle, it was her sister's face that caught her attention. Julie grinned. It was a mad and desperate spreading of lips and baring of teeth.

"You noticed, didn't you?" she whispered.

Val tensed but forced herself to start walking again.

Julie was quick to stay close at her side. "You've always been bright. You noticed."

"Noticed what?" Felix asked, holding Julie by the arm to keep her from tripping in the overgrowth.

Val let out a breath and the answer. "He didn't limp when he crossed the river."

Julie laughed, struggling to keep her voice low for the sake of secrecy.

"Adrenaline, maybe? He can't be faking a knife wound. Calvin stitched it up," Felix whispered, words rushed as they were catching up with the others.

Julie didn't pay him any attention, shoulder bumping into Val's as they walked. "What else have you noticed, Val?"

Val bit her lip to resist answering.

"Have you noticed that it's quiet?"

Val scrunched her brow and turned to look back at her sister before slowly looking around at the trees. There were birds in the branches high above, and even a few small capuchin monkeys, but none of them made any sounds. In fact, they had stopped whatever lively game they usually played and turned their heads down to watch with beady black eyes as the group cut through the jungle.

For the first time since she dragged herself onto this island, it was quiet.

No chirping, no cawing, no howling or screeching. Not a single damned sound in all that jungle life around them.

"He's not him," Julie said again, the words firmer now, as though they'd meant something obvious all along.

Chapter 16

Val pushed her way forward through the group. Maeko sneered but didn't get a chance to say anything before Val was well past her and Poppy and coming up on Lochner and Zach. Just as she reached out to grab his shoulder, bent on getting answers to questions she hadn't yet formed, Zach tripped. He stumbled forward and somehow twisted to the side so that Lochner couldn't catch him in time. He fell hard into Henry's back. The cameraman let out a wail of fright, knees buckling and body falling hard under Zach's.

Calvin turned in surprise, his focus previously fixed on navigating their path. His eyes widened when he saw the two men on the ground, but Lochner was already grabbing Zach and lifting him to his feet again. Zach let out a huff and apologized.

Val hurried to help up Henry. He looked dazed and hurt, groping at his chest where the shape of Megan's camera had creased his shirt and likely bruised his skin. The camera itself had been crushed beneath their fall, now pancaked on the jungle floor. He pushed away from Val's help to kneel in front of it, scooping up the mass of cracked plastic and broken glass. He turned it over in his hands and tried to turn it on. Nothing happened when he jabbed the buttons. No lights. No screen. No reeling sound of the technology struggling to work. It was wrecked.

"Sorry," Zach muttered, still trying to recover from the fall himself and leaning into a tree.

Val turned from Henry to look at Zach. He favored his good leg dramatically now, and she couldn't help but feel suspicious. Had he run into Henry on purpose, or was it really just an accident? Was there something on the camera that he didn't want them to see? She'd watched all of the footage on it already, but he couldn't know that. There was nothing she could think of worth worrying about except for Megan's death. Except for the static figure that attacked her. She felt cold even in the heat of the jungle morning. What if he didn't know it had been static? What if he didn't know something had been wrong with her camera and feared he'd been caught on film? But was she really going to assume he was a murderer because he ruined a camera?

Zach stared back at her, and for a fraction of a second, his eyes weren't his. His mouth twitched with a smile, and the darkness of his pupils expanded, looking at her and into her, reaching for her. She jerked back and would have fallen on her ass if Calvin hadn't been standing so close to help Henry. He caught her arm and gave her a funny look.

"You okay?" Calvin sounded more frustrated than worried at this point. She could sympathize. They were so close to ending this nightmare. So close, that not making it had suddenly become more dreadful than ever.

Val blinked back at Zach, but his eyes were normal now and his face creased with worry. "Are you okay, Val?" He repeated Calvin's question, words dripping with concern. He didn't look well, but he wasn't a monster. He was pale and gray from blood loss and exhaustion. The bags under his eyes were like dark bruises, and his lips were the same drawn color as his cheeks. He rubbed at his ear when it began to bleed but didn't mention any pain. It was the same as his nosebleed, a casual nuisance.

She swallowed hard at a growing lump in her throat but nodded. It was impossible not to think back to the jaguar on the stream, bleeding from nose, ears, and eyes. What if they were sick? This place had been quarantined long ago. What if they had somehow contracted a disease? What if she had it now, too? She straightened, and eventually Calvin let go of her arm, turning his attention back to Henry.

The cameraman was still on the ground fussing over what was now little more than a heap of broken plastic.

"Fuck man. Just take the memory card and leave the rest behind. We need to keep moving," Calvin said firmly.

When Henry just sat there, he crouched down and took the camera from his hands. Calvin pulled out the memory card and handed it to Henry before tossing the camera off into the bushes. "Let's go." He grabbed the other man's arms and made him stand. "Are you hurt?" he asked, words clear and as patient as he could manage.

Henry shook his head.

Calvin clapped his shoulders and then let him go. "Start walking."

Lochner offered Zach an arm and helped him hobble through the jungle after Calvin. Val watched them go, followed by the others until she stood alone with Felix and

Julie again. Her sister didn't say anything this time, but the way she stared at her was so terribly smug and certain that it left Val feeling all the more unsure of herself.

"I think they might be sick," Val whispered to Felix when they, too, started walking. "Zach has been having nosebleeds, and now he's bleeding from the ears."

She turned her head to look at her sister, studying her. Julie was a mess, but she didn't look as bad as Zach. Then again, she wasn't the one who got stabbed.

"Has she had anything like that?" Val asked her husband while studying her sister.

Felix shook his head. "No. Nothing I've seen."

Val went quiet for a few minutes while they walked, trying to decide how to explain what she saw, or what she thought she saw.

Felix sensed her tension and touched her back with his free hand, the one not holding Julie's leash. "What else?" he asked, voice low in case it was a secret.

Val cringed. "I might be hallucinating," she admitted just as quietly.

He shrugged casually. "You're hungry and tired, and you've been running on adrenaline the last few days. I think a little hallucination at this point is okay."

Val nodded, liking the sound of his reasoning. "Let me know if I'm acting weird," she added quickly, looking at Julie one more time.

They walked for another two hours. Lochner was certain that the rescue team would have to transport them to the capital city since none of the villages between the coastline and the city would have adequate hospitals. Poppy was already planning her first meal once they reached the mainland. For about ten minutes, conversation devolved into a list of meat dishes she couldn't decide between and, in the end, decided to get all of them. Maeko finally told her to shut up when she couldn't take the reminder of how empty her own stomach was anymore. Val suspected everyone was a little grateful, even if Maeko was harsh with her choice of words.

They still had some protein bars, jerky, and meal packs left from the land team's supplies, but they'd been sparing in their last meal and decided to save the rest for when they made camp. What had been meant for four people was now being shared between nine.

When they came to another stream, the group greeted it happily. They hadn't stopped to drink from the last one, wanting to move away from the bone bridge as quickly as possible, and their water bottles had all been empty for a while.

"Refill and drink, and then let's keep moving," Calvin said, eager to get to the beach by nightfall.

Maeko nodded, taking off her backpack to fish out the empty plastic bottle. She frowned sharply at Henry when he sat down on the grass near the edge of the water. Poppy pretended not to see Maeko's glare and sat next to him. She dipped her arms in the water and washed her face.

"This isn't a spa, Poppy. Drink and get up," Maeko snapped.

Poppy looked up, surprised first, and then annoyed. "Excuse me?"

Calvin groaned. "Five minutes," he said, like a parent to two children. "Do what you want, but in five minutes we're moving along." He walked into the stream and across it. It came up to his knees at its deepest, the bank on the other side a little muddy, making the crossing less than graceful.

Lochner followed, and so did Maeko, eager to get the

others moving, too. Luckily, no one was paying her any attention, as they had all decided to go with Calvin's five-minute rest.

Julie squirmed against her ropes, movements sluggish with exhaustion. "Can I wash up before we keep going?" she asked, looking up at Felix.

His brow pinched in discomfort, hesitating to deny her freedom when she had been quiet and following along so easily the past couple hours. He turned to Val, waiting for a signal from her.

Val filled up the water bottle she'd taken from her pack and then came over and handed the plastic container to Felix in exchange for the rope. Julie turned away from her and held her arms out from her back.

Val picked at the knot. "If you run, we'll chase you down, Jules. I'm not leaving this island without you."

"You're not leaving this island at all," she mumbled, sounding more bitter and tired now than before.

Val groaned and shook her head. "It's shit like that that makes me unsure about untying you," she admitted. The rope came loose, and she grabbed Julie's arm to make her turn toward her before she went to the stream. "Don't attack anyone."

Julie stared back at her for another few seconds before finally nodding. "Fine." She went to kneel at the water's edge.

Val watched over her sister for a minute or two before noticing that Zach still hadn't joined them at the stream. He walked along the side of the bank, craning his neck to see down its length.

"Everything okay?" Val finally called. Felix and a few others took notice of Zach then.

He shifted about between his hurt leg and his good

one, twisting to look back at them but pointing down-stream. "This curves down to the beach. We could just follow it, that way we don't run out of water," he said.

Calvin scrunched his face and took a handful of steps in Zach's direction, along the other side of the stream. "Don't worry about it. There are streams all over this is-land. We're cutting a straight line to the beach."

"It's been five minutes," Maeko pressed, voice low and urgent.

Poppy stood, brushing off her legs before helping up Henry. Together, they crossed the stream.

"I think this could be a shortcut!" Zach insisted, still standing downstream and making no move to come back to them.

Felix bent down to refill the bottle he'd drained and then capped it. He came around to Val's back and un-zipped her pack to put the water bottle away. "Let's go, Zach!" he called, tired and sweaty like everyone else.

Zach still didn't budge, shifting about uneasily on his legs.

Julie stood up, and Val snapped her attention to the side to make sure her sister wasn't up to anything. Julie stood still, staring right at her. "I don't think he can cross water," she said casually.

Val scrunched her brow. "What?" She looked back down the stream at Zach. He looked anxious, squirming in his own skin. Maybe whatever illness he had was similar to rabies. She took one step toward Zach, intent on bring-ing him over the stream one way or another. She was de-termined to get them rescued and to a hospital as fast as possible.

Julie caught her by the arm, and for a moment she looked like herself. Tired, and dirty, and brokenhearted, but herself. "Val," Julie said softly, tears in her eyes. "I'm sorry."

Val felt her chest tighten with dread. "For what?"

"For bringing you here. For bringing Felix here." She dragged in a deep breath and then let it out shakily. "And for not having killed you before things got worse."

Maeko let out a scream. She backpedaled into the stream, her elbow locked and arm pointed high.

Val barely had time to look up and see the branches heavy with silent, black howler monkeys before one let loose a deafening sound. The others burst from the branches, hitting the ground hard and running at the travelers.

Chapter 17

Henry was the first to move, bolting into the trees. Lochner called after him and followed, a troop of howlers barreling through the bushes in chase.

Before anyone could think better of it, they all started running. Some fled, and others followed. The monkeys in the trees echoed that terrible siren howl, making Val's heart hammer in her chest until her ears throbbed.

She darted across the river to follow Lochner and Henry. Her muscles ached, and her mind screamed, chasing those wild animals through the jungle. Half her instincts begged her to stop, to flee in another direction, but those wild animals were already chasing someone else, and she couldn't leave them on their own.

The sounds only got louder the closer they came, the monkeys jumping and screaming on the ground. It wasn't until she was on them that she realized one of those screams was very human. The howlers were jumping on top of someone, beating down their fists and mashing their faces into the core of the pile.

She dug into her pocket and pulled out her knife,

flipping it open with her thumb and lunging in at the mound of black fur and limbs. It made her skin burn and her heart pound inside her chest so hard that her vision blurred. Instincts raged for her to run, and actually grabbing at the animals sent jolts of terror through her limbs. But she could see Lochner under them. She could see his bloody chest and one of his arms lying limp on the ground.

She pulled and kicked, and when the monkeys finally turned on her, she stabbed with her little knife. The metal sunk into the side of a chest, scraping at ribs and eliciting a nearly human cry of pain. Val realized in a gut-twisting flash of thought that it was the first time she'd ever stabbed any living thing.

The monkey swung at her, smacking her back and nearly off her feet. She hit a tree trunk. Her vision grew too bright and unfocused for a second but came back in time to see those blood-slick teeth bared in her direction. The monkey turned his back on her and drove his face and all those teeth down into Lochner. He didn't scream anymore.

Tears clouded her eyes, but Val pushed off the tree. Her whole body ached, shaking, but nothing seemed broken. She rolled her shoulders to drop her pack down and held it by one strap. She swung hard and smacked one of the monkeys off of him and then used it as a shield to press another back while she stabbed at the last. She slashed when they lunged at her, cutting right across a face before another leaped out at her from the side.

Teeth sunk into her arm, and a scream rose from her chest, bursting from her throat. It wasn't so much the pain at that moment as it was the sickly sensation of long fangs striking one of the bones in her forearm and sliding off.

Her knees hit the ground beside Lochner during the

scuffle, kicking one monkey back before stabbing down at the head attached to her arm. The blade sank into that smaller skull, the teeth pushing deeper into her arm before they both collapsed.

The other monkeys scrambled away into the foliage, climbing up trees and then jumping from branch to branch to flee the scene. Leaves fell like rain all around them.

"Kevin!" Calvin shouted, and for one strange moment, Val was confused. And then he rushed past her and dropped to the ground beside Lochner's body. Kevin Lochner. The name was so easy to forget when no one used it. His eyes were open and his face mauled. His throat gaped, supplying a lake of blood to wet the earth beneath him. He was dead.

Calvin struggled to breathe, pulling at Lochner's body, wrapping his arms around him.

Val gasped and panted for air, kicking at the ground to sit up, a monkey still latched onto her arm though the animal was very much dead. She cringed and reached out, grabbing at its face with bloody fingers and pulling until those teeth finally started to slide out of her skin. She screamed in pain but kept pulling until they finally came out completely. Angrily, she kicked the dead thing away.

Dark blood pushed up from big holes in her skin, wetting her clothes. She grabbed at her pack, dragging it to her and unzipping it with one hand. Every so often she looked at Calvin, keeping an eye on him while he mourned. She grabbed the water from her bag, quickly rinsing off her arm before digging out one of the t-shirts she'd saved from Julie's things. She wrapped it around her forearm. The bright blue cotton soaked up red until it became a deep purple. She used her teeth to help tie it off and then forced herself to her feet.

"Calvin," she said his name, breathing hard and looking around the jungle. She could hear someone shouting. She shouldered the backpack and then grabbed the handle of her knife again, jerking it twice before it came free of the monkeys head.

"Please, Cal," Val pleaded, adrenaline alone keeping her on her feet now. "We need to find the others," she continued, reaching out to touch his shoulder, fingers twisting in his t-shirt. Someone was definitely screaming somewhere nearby in the jungle, but no matter how her eyes squinted, she couldn't see through all the trees, branches, and vines.

"Calvin, we have to move," she begged now because she couldn't leave him behind no matter how her heart longed to find Felix and Julie.

He sucked in a deep breath that shook his whole body and nodded. He swallowed hard, and even she could hear it.

He picked up the large knife Lochner had dropped and crawled to his feet.

Val awkwardly held onto his shirt and started pulling, dragging him those first few steps toward the sounds of others before they fell into a jog and she let go. He followed, and she was grateful because she wasn't sure she'd chase him now if he ran off on his own.

Maeko barreled into them, her screams cut off by the impact. Val cringed when the woman grabbed at her wounded arm. Maeko's wild eyes focused on her before shoving her back a step. She twisted around to look back at what Val assumed had been howler's chasing her through the jungle. Leaves fell from the trees as dark shapes climbed back up to safety.

"Where are the others?" Val asked. "Where's Felix?"

Maeko panted and stared at her. She took them both in, one at a time, and then her gaze locked on to the knife in Calvin's hand. Her whole body tensed, turning toward him. Calvin looked confused for a split second before Maeko lunged at him. She jerked to the side to jab her shoulder into his chest. A gush of air pushed up from his lungs while both of her hands latched onto his wrist, her body tangling with his to tackle him to the ground.

Val grabbed at her shoulder, but Maeko only started screaming, one hand still trying to pry the knife from Calvin's grip while her other arm beat down against his face. Calvin raised his free arm between them, trying to push her back. His other arm was rigid, locked at the elbow; he was afraid to move it and risk stabbing her.

Biting her lip, Val folded her knife and shoved it down into her jeans pocket. She hissed in pain when she moved her hurt arm, grabbing a fistful of the other woman's hair. Her other arm reached down again, grabbing at Maeko's face and pulling until they both fell away from Calvin onto the ground.

Before Val could think of what to do next, Maeko twisted around on top of her. The other woman sat on her chest, lifted her head in both hands, and slammed the back of her skull against the jungle floor. Her vision swam, the sounds of impact echoing between her ears.

Maeko was rabid, flailing and striking out at her, but Val couldn't feel it. Maeko grabbed at the strap of Val's backpack, focusing in on it and pulling violently. She stood just enough to keep pulling and force Val to flip over so that she could start peeling it off of her.

"Maeko..." Val tried, voice tight with pain when her wounded arm smacked down against the ground. "Wait."

Maeko kicked her hard in the back and stumbled away with the backpack, clutching it to her chest like the last parachute on a plane spiraling toward the ground.

Calvin was up again, and the knife she'd previously coveted caught a glint of sunlight through the trees. "Maeko." He said her name roughly, coughing it out. His eyes were bloodshot and teary from Lochner's death, and his lip bled from Maeko's fit. He held out his empty hand toward her, fingers spread in an attempt to calm her. He held the knife back and away from her, trying not to threaten her with it though he obviously wasn't going to put it down.

Maeko shuddered, clinging to the backpack. "Give me the knife." The words tore up from her chest, trembling like the rest of her, not from cold or fright, but from desperation. "I need it."

Calvin shook his head, her madness seemed to lend him clarity. "We need to find the others."

"Fuck the others!" Maeko screamed. "I'm not staying! I'm not dying with you!"

Val climbed back to her feet, her left arm curled against her chest and bleeding through the blue shirt turned bandage. "Maeko—" she tried again.

"Shut up!" the woman screamed, shuffling a few steps back, hugging the pack tight to her chest. When she turned and started to run, Val chased her. She wasn't sure herself if it was over the supplies in the bag, to stop her from getting lost, or just to put the rushing of her pulse to work. Calvin called after them.

Val latched onto Maeko's shoulder with her right hand. Her left arm pressed into her chest again, every movement jolting pain through that ravaged flesh. She pulled, trying to make Maeko stop, but instead she tripped, and they both tumbled down a short dip in the ground. Val blacked out from the pain shooting like lightning through her arm when she rolled over it. It throbbed out waves of agony, and for a moment she forgot everything else, every other bruise and cut, every nightmarish thing that had happened on this island. For a moment, the world was quiet and she was someplace else.

When she opened her eyes again, she blinked up at branches, her back to the hard ground. A fat leaf wobbled over her face. It looked plastic and impossibly green.

Calvin came to stand over her, talking and talking, but for the longest time, he didn't make any sound—as though the world was on mute. She blinked and watched him pant and shout. She could see in his eyes that he was asking her questions, but she couldn't hear anything until the ringing slowly started. Quiet at first and building until it was so loud that she cringed, and then, like a balloon popping, the sounds of the world flooded back to her.

When she sat up, Calvin knelt beside her and helped hold her upright while the world spun.

"We have to go. We have to find the others," he said, and she found herself nodding when he pulled her to her feet. It was then that she noticed her pack, the one Maeko had stolen, was on his back.

Val continued nodding. Yes, they had to go. They had to find the others. She turned to convey this certainty to Maeko, but the other woman hadn't gotten up. She was sprawled on the jungle ground, not unlike the way Val had been. Her eyes were open and her lips parted just the slightest bit, as though she was inhaling to speak, but she wasn't inhaling at all. She had a rock for a pillow, and a skull reshaped to fit it like a puzzle piece.

Val felt sick, her body trying to turn back to Maeko,

but Calvin pulled her up the hill by her good arm. He pushed off trees for leverage, calling out names. Felix, Poppy, Julie, Zach, Henry. He called them loud, one after another. No more Maeko. No more Lochner.

She tried to look back again when they got to the top of that steep hill. The jungle had closed in behind them, too much lush green and thick glossy leaves to make out anything on the ground. She couldn't see Maeko. Her hands shook. She'd killed her. She felt sick, mostly because it could just as easily have been her head smashed into that rock.

Calvin wasn't playing nursemaid. He let go of her arm when she kept a pace of her own and continued to shout names. He shouted them like they were just sounds, without meaning or people attached to them. She looked at him, his face red and sweaty and his eyes swollen from tears. He cupped his hands and howled another name, another cry of pain and anger raging up from his lungs. They weren't names at all. They were just a means to scream.

Chapter 18

They found Julie first—not that she answered their calls, but they happened upon her in the jungle.

Val grabbed her hand and looked her over quickly. She looked as bad as she did before the attack. "Are you okay?"

Julie looked around, tugging Val along if she insisted on clinging to her hand. "He ran off this way," she mumbled, pointing at the ground and the thick drops of blood there. "The jungle won't let him go. Won't let any of us go," she continued, voice quiet but certain.

Val hissed angrily but followed her sister. "Yes, I'm great, thanks for fucking asking, Jules!" she snapped before clawing bloody fingers over her scalp to push her hair out of her face.

She and Calvin followed Julie down the stream until they heard voices through the trees. Val's heart leaped to her throat when she pushed through the thick foliage and into a short clearing. The land on the other end of that clearing dropped off, the river collapsing into a waterfall she could hear even from where she stood. Poppy, Felix, and Zach gathered there, not far from the edge, arguing.

Felix pointed back toward the trees, and Zach pointed in the other direction, off the edge of the cliff and down toward the jungle beneath. In the distance, from that height, Val could see a glimpse of the beach and a stretch of blue ocean against the horizon.

"Felix!" Val shouted, rushing those last yards to him.

His body whipped around at the sound of her voice, and she saw the whole spectrum of emotions move across his features. He met her with open arms. His hand cradled her head to his chest when he kissed her hair, whispering a prayer.

"Where are the others?" Poppy asked, hope mingling with dread in her voice.

Calvin just shook his head, pretending not to see when she started to cry. "What happened to you?" he asked Zach instead, and Val looked up, as well. Blood oozed from his eyes like dark tears.

"I think he's sick," Felix offered, distracted with Val's arm as he started unwrapping the blood-soaked t-shirt to get a look at it. "How did this happen? Is this a bite?"

Val winced. It was still bleeding a lot. They were going to have to stitch and bandage it soon. "Monkey."

Felix looked up at her, a funny, morbid smile playing at the corner of his mouth. "What's with you and getting this arm eaten?"

"It didn't eat me," she protested, almost too tired and dizzy to bother. "It bit me." She blanched when she thought of Lochner but swallowed back anything she wanted to tell Felix about it while Calvin was still close by.

Felix looked unconvinced but turned toward Calvin. "Is that Val's bag? I think it has some of the first aid supplies."

Calvin nodded and took those two steps back to them,

shrugging off the bag. He was about to unzip it when Julie rushed past him. Her sprint turned into a lunge, legs pushing off the ground to launch her shoulder into Zach's chest.

Val couldn't even get out a scream before her sister tackled him right off the edge of the cliff. They vanished from sight completely, and for one second, Val was certain it was the worst thing she'd ever seen. They were there, and then they were gone, and her heart felt like it had been crushed inside her chest.

A moment of stillness swelled in their absence just before they all rushed forward. Poppy and Calvin were first to the edge, leaning over the side of rock and falling water, staring at the small lake below.

Val was already half climbing, half falling, down the slope alongside the waterfall. "Julie!" she shouted, head whipping back and forth between watching her step and looking to the water to see if her sister had come up yet.

She was almost to the bottom when the surface broke. Zach's body popped up. He floated face-up with blood dripping thickly from his eyes, nose, and ears to spread out, dark and inky, into the water around him.

One fat crocodile slid off the bank and disappeared beneath the water. Another bobbed up from below, the crown of scales on its head and snout hinting to its size.

Julie was much louder when she surfaced, gasping at a swallow of air and looking around for Zach. She only had to swim a few strokes to reach him, but something had changed in her now that he was dead. She didn't attack him. She let out a sob and grabbed onto Zach's corpse. She hugged him and cried louder. She mumbled "I love you" repeatedly and pushed her face into the side of his, rocking against him.

The water rippled all around them when the crocodiles moved closer, and Val's throat burned for the volume of her screams. She watched those ripples draw closer and closer to her sister in the water. She cried out her name, begging her to swim, but Julie only clung to Zach, hugging him tightly and closing her eyes.

Val was two steps into the water when Felix scooped her up from behind. He held her back to his chest, arms around her waist to lift her feet off the ground. She reached out with bloody hands and screamed when the crocodiles struck, pulling her sister underwater first, and then another pair rushed in to fight over Zach's corpse.

It was like the moment she fell off the ledge all over again. Her sister was there, and then she was gone. Only now, Val couldn't follow.

Chapter 19

Val stared at her arm. The alcohol washed the blood away from the floppy folds of torn flesh but more came up. There was always more blood. She watched the needle push against one edge of skin and then cross the wound to come up out the other side. It pulled, and the thick black thread followed, dragging through her skin, tugging the two sides together again. Felix could sew it up, but it wouldn't be the same. Those stitches, tying up the holes made by thick teeth, crossed paths with older scars made by triangular serrated teeth.

She had been bitten by two animals now, but the only one she could think about was the one that had bitten her sister. If she didn't know better, she could tell herself that death came instantly, but experience and knowledge told her that Julie had probably drowned, dragged down in that murky water with teeth deep in her flesh and the weight of jaws bearing down on her. Where had the crocodile bitten her first? A leg? Her torso? Did she struggle and try to get free or did she take a big gulp of water into her lungs and welcome death?

Welcoming death didn't seem right. It didn't seem like Julie. But nothing today had seemed like Julie. Nothing until that last moment, when she surfaced and grabbed onto Zach. When she mourned him as though she hadn't killed him, as though she'd only just found him.

Val closed her eyes. She felt hollow and the world felt slow. The sounds of the jungle returned, distant and timid now, as though the creatures of this damned place were embarrassed about their part in it all.

Felix rolled the bandage around her arm, dressing it from wrist to elbow.

Daylight faded fast between the trees, and Poppy set up one of the two tents they had. She crawled inside, zipped it up, and cried. Val and Felix pretended not to hear her because it was the closest thing to privacy she could find, and after today, no one was going to take it from her.

Calvin sat himself down and pulled his legs up against his chest. His forehead pressed to his knees, one arm locked around his legs, and the other hand buried in his hair, clawing at his skull. Every so often his breathing grew quick, rushed, heavy, but he didn't cry like Poppy in the tent. He just sat there, as still as he could, not looking at anyone or anything.

Felix didn't ask about Lochner. He didn't have to. And he didn't ask Calvin to stitch up her arm either. He had tried it once or twice himself and seen it done a dozen times more. He just sat her down near the others, held out her arm, and went to work. Val expected to feel it. She had hoped the needle and the pain would wake her, but it didn't, and she suspected nothing would.

Julie was dead.

Eaten.

They were never going to get off of the island.

When her hand felt warm, Val blinked and looked down at it. Felix held her hand between both of his. Her scars and missing digit disappeared under his warm skin. A tear burned hot down her cheek when she looked up at him; a lump caught in her throat, threatening to strangle her.

"You promised," he said softly, and she watched his mouth when he spoke. "You're going to get us off this island, remember? You're going to save me." His mouth curved into a beautiful smile, and that lump rolled up from her throat, uncorking her misery like a bottle of wine. She sobbed and leaned forward, his arms wrapping around her. She wished he could hide all of her the way he could envelop her hand. She wished, even just for a little while, that she could vanish and be anywhere—absolutely anywhere—but on that island.

Chapter 20

Even when daylight faded completely, sinking them into a consuming darkness, Val wouldn't crawl into the tent Felix had set up.

Poppy was still tucked away in hers, having fallen asleep. It had taken some time, but Felix eventually convinced Calvin to move into the second tent and get some rest. When he settled in, Felix returned to Val, touching her arms carefully and leaning into her sight. He urged her to sleep. He urged her to share Poppy's tent until the sun came up again, but she wouldn't go. She wouldn't crawl into that nylon bag and pretend that she was safe.

The jungle didn't sleep. How could she?

Felix eventually relented, but he never got into a tent himself. He sat with his back to hers so they could watch in both directions and wait for dawn. She listened to his breathing and felt it through her back. She watched the dark trees, waiting, always waiting.

Felix's breathing changed when he fell asleep. She would know it anywhere after years of sharing a bed. Her heart felt like a stone in her chest. Sadness upon sadness and fear piled upon that. She swallowed hard at the lump in her throat, worrying that this would be the last time she heard him sleep. How much longer could she keep them alive? Did she really still believe they would reach the beach? That the rescue would arrive and whisk them away from this place? That there was any place in the world where she would feel safe again?

A twig broke in the darkness ahead, and she stared into the night. Her thumb pushed the button of the flashlight against her hip, and bright light flared to life, making her squint. The shadows became a thousand times more sinister for that light, pouring into the darkness but unable to conquer it. She ran the beam of light over the trees. Two green eyes shone back, bright and large.

The jaguar sat in the thick leaves, tail flicking back and forth. Its head tipped to one side as it stared at her. She waited for it to leap or rush forward or even slip away into the dark jungle to play games with her sanity. For minutes that felt like hours, they stared at one another. The large cat stood up and wandered closer, unbothered by the beam of light or the woman watching. It walked into their little makeshift camp. It circled Poppy's tent, sniffing at the nylon, whiskers scraping against the thin material. Every so often, its large head rolled to the side, looking back at Val. She watched it snort with disinterest and then move on to consider Calvin's tent, bringing itself ever closer to her.

Its heavy paws pressed down grass and dirt. Its shoulders shifted with each step, violently alive beneath short fur and thick skin. When it was done with Calvin's tent, it came around to her. She could tell by the trajectory of its steps that it meant to circle her and Felix next, and suddenly, for the first time, fear rose up in her chest at the idea of it being at her back with Felix where she could no longer see it.

Before she could move or speak, the cat stopped. It stood in the shadows to the side of her and her light and stared back. That tail flicked one last time, ever thoughtful and full of decision, and then the great cat turned away and walked back into the jungle. She continued to stare at that spot in the trees long after it had gone, watching the darkness even after she pushed the button on her flash-light to let the night sweep back in, consuming her again.

For long minutes after the cat had gone, there was on-ly silence. No birds or insects or distant cries. Only dread-ful silence.

And then, slowly, the jungle life stirred again in the trees all around them, whispering and laughing. She sat there and felt like the only silent, still thing in a cacophony of life. She didn't sleep. She wouldn't. She just waited, for the sun to come up or for the trees to go silent again.

Chapter 21

They were slow to rise in the morning. Val saw the sunrise as well as anyone could see it in the depths of a forest. It came in the changing of shades and the rising of light, in the colors that came to life, in the shift in sounds and temperature, and in the opening of flowers.

She considered, sitting alone surrounded by what was left of her traveling party, letting them sleep as long as they could. Despair told her to give that to them, to let them have these last moments of peace before what could very well be their final day. It was the last despairing thought she allowed herself. It was the last moment of the night turning to morning that she gave in to grief and fear. When it passed, she stood, turning to catch Felix's shoulder with her good hand and give it a squeeze.

She bent down and kissed his cheek. "Time to wake up. I have to save you today." She gave him a little shake and heard him mutter a sloppy reply, too tired to be witty but not too tired to appreciate her words.

She let him go, and he stretched where he sat, rubbing at his face.

She woke Poppy and then Calvin. She drew them from their tents and let Poppy take up the task of emptying their two bags to see what food they had left. "Divide it up and eat," Val decided for them all, and no one argued. They would need the energy to make it to the beach. After that, it would just be a matter of waiting for the rescue. Calvin wasn't saying anything. He just sat there, staring at the ground. "We'll get to the beach today," Val continued, collapsing and folding up one of the tents.

Poppy looked up, having just broken a protein bar into quarters. "We're not lost?" she asked, voice raw and eyelids swollen from crying the night before.

Val shook her head. "We know which way the beach is. We'll make it before afternoon."

Felix stuffed the second tent into one of the bags Poppy had already emptied.

"Do we have to keep moving?" Poppy asked, pulling the last of the jerky from another bag to start dividing it into the four piles she was making.

Val nodded, hugging the rolled-up tent and bringing it over. Felix grabbed up the second bag and held it open for her to push it in. "It'll be easier for them to get to us and faster for getting off the island. And we should be safer on the beach. We can keep an eye on the jungle better."

Poppy looked worried but nodded, handing Felix and Val their fistfuls of breakfast. When she held out Calvin's, he didn't seem to notice. His head was down and his mouth moving, whispering, but none of them could hear what he was saying. He shuddered and closed his eyes, cringing.

Poppy reached out with her other hand to grab onto his shoulder. She squeezed gently. "Calvin?" His eyes opened so suddenly that Poppy let go of him and jerked back.

He sucked in a deep breath, as though filling himself all the way down to his toes, and then finally relaxed. His shoulders eased back when he let out that breath, and his head lifted to look around. He blinked back at them with a terrible calm, familiar, but not something Val had ever seen on him before.

Poppy tried again, holding out the food in her palm. "A-are you hungry?" she asked, more worried now than ever.

He looked at the offering and then smiled. "Thanks." He reached out with cupped hands, and she dumped the jerky and bits of protein bar into his palms. They sat quietly and ate. It didn't take long to finish all the food they had left and drain the two water bottles.

Calvin stood and stretched when he finished, and Val watched him carefully. Maybe he was in shock. It was as though all grief and fear had drained out of him and a new energy was fueled by that meager breakfast. He offered to carry one of the packs, and Felix smiled, glad to see him snapping out of it even if just for a while. Felix carried the second himself, and Val led the way through the trees. They didn't have to rush today. They would make it well before sundown, even at a casual pace.

Poppy kept close to her side, talking about the rescue team, wondering if they would go back for the bodies, and if they would have boats or helicopters. She talked faster than she could think, and Val didn't bother to listen to most of it, knowing that it was mostly just to calm herself with the sound of it.

The day quickly grew hot, warmer than any of the days before. There was barely any direct sunlight with the trees so thick around them, but that shade didn't offer any reprieve from the heat; in fact, it made the air wet and heavy all around them.

Val turned to look back to check on the guys. Calvin was staring at her, his eyes darker than she remembered, with bags beneath them. He didn't look away when their eyes locked, looking back at her without smiling or speaking. The skin on her neck and spine tightened beneath a bead of sweat rolling down her back.

When Poppy quieted, Val realized that the other woman was pointing out something in the branches high and to the right. Val looked up, a rise of panic in her chest at the anticipation of more howler monkeys. Her steps fell to a stop when she saw the mass of butterflies clinging to the side of a tree, clustered together to bask in a beam of sunlight. Their wings moved slowly, opening and closing, flashing bright blue.

Poppy let out a sigh. "Too bad we don't have any cameras left," she muttered distantly.

Val nodded along, but she remembered a camera. She'd put it in one of the bags. She started walking again, leading them down a slope that grew so steep they had to walk sideways. Val took that time to try to remember which bag the camera was in. It had been in hers to start with, and that meant it was one of the two with them now. The question was whether it was on Felix or Calvin's back.

She looked around at the trees as they walked, now on flat ground once more. They hadn't crossed a stream all day, loosely following the river from the falls toward the ocean. She found herself going through Julie's last day as they walked. She had repeated again and again that Zach wasn't Zach. She'd said that he couldn't cross the water, and the only time Val had seen him walk over a stream all that day had been on the bones of the island's victims.

She could hear the river to their left.

The toe of her shoe kicked up a clump of grass when she stopped and turned, looking around at the softer ground and smooth rocks. "We should take a break."

Felix looked surprised, but Poppy exhaled in relief. She found the closest, softest-looking spot and sat down.

Val came around to Felix's back and opened the pack there before he could take it off. She pulled out the water bottle and then rummaged around for the camera. Her heart beat faster. Was she really doing this? Was she really suspicious just because Calvin calmed down? So had she, hadn't she? The camera wasn't in Felix's bag, which meant that it was in Calvin's.

"I'll go down and get us some water." She zipped it up and walked around Felix to see Calvin already opening up his backpack on the ground to find the empty plastic bottle.

"We should stick together," Felix said uneasily. He could sense that there was something up, his deep brown eyes studying her for his queue.

"Rest," Val said, coming over to Calvin. He held out the bottle for her, not offering to go with her to the river. It wasn't like him, but it wasn't exactly damnable either.

"Cal can go with me," she said, staring back at him and making no move to take the bottle.

His arm locked, still holding it out for another second before he smiled and shrugged. He pulled it back to himself and dropped his bag with Poppy. "We'll be back," Calvin said, walking away toward the sound of the river.

Val watched him for a second longer before grabbing up his bag and digging out the camera. She held it in her palm and hurried after him.

Her skin felt raw when she trailed him, stalking him. An empty water bottle in one hand and a camera in the other. The shape of her pocket knife burned her hip, but she had no free hand left to take it out.

"Sorry to make you come with," Val spoke up, thumb pushing at the button on the small camera to bring it to life, the shield on the lens sliding out of place. "I just thought Poppy and Felix were looking burned out and I know you've done a lot of hiking before."

Calvin nodded, moving down a rocky edge of land, closer and closer to the river. They could see it now, emerald and fast, cutting through the trees ahead. "Sure."

She changed the settings on the camera to have it film rather than take pictures.

"How are you doing? You haven't said much since—" She almost choked on the name. Reminding him would be cruel. She wouldn't do that to him if she wasn't suspicious. But suspicious of what? "Lochner," she said his name and watched Calvin's shoulders. She expected them to tense. She expected him to look back. She expected some sign of misery or anger.

"I'm tired," Calvin said, not sounding it at all. "Aren't you getting tired?"

She held up the camera, the lens focusing on him and the trees around. He wasn't a shadow or a distortion like the ones they'd seen on the footage of Megan's camera. She let out a little breath of relief, mouth pulling into a smile and eyes welling with tears. It had been a camera malfunction. She was acting crazy. On impulse alone, she clicked the button to start the recording. The image jumped when the red light came on, and his shape became a dark smear in the middle of the small screen. Relief choked in her throat, and when she looked up from the camera, Calvin was looking back at her.

He waited while she slowly dropped her arm back to

her side. The camera fell from her fingers to land in the grass. She felt sick. She wanted to run, but she didn't dare. Megan had run.

"Who are you?" Val whispered.

Some part of her hoped that he would deny it.

"Oh, don't tell me you're going to lose it like your sister now?" He smiled wide with too much amusement, threatening the corners of his mouth.

"You're not Calvin. What are you?" It was almost a plea. Her newly emptied hand twitched, fingers eager to dig the knife out of her pocket and at least feel a little safer.

He let out an annoyed sigh but didn't quite lose his smile. He looked around, and Val still hoped that he would be Calvin, that he would be annoyed and pissed the way the man she'd known would be. She wanted him to rake his fingers through his hair in frustration and tell her to fuck off the way he usually would.

When he was done glancing through the trees to make sure they were alone, he fell still. Completely, eerily still. His head rolled to one side and looked back at her, and she remembered the jaguar the night before, studying them one by one. "It would be a waste of breath in this corpse to explain to you," Calvin replied with a grin.

Val shuddered, her knees locking to keep her from falling. "You killed Zach," she accused, lungs pushing out the first words she could gather up.

His mouth pulled more, as though he was laughing, but no sound came to fill the wide shape of his lips. "Your sister killed Zach. I could have stayed in that body for at least another day or two before it fell apart."

Val was glad she locked her knees because she would have fallen on her ass then. Her breaths came in tight, her mind reeling, trying to believe while at the same time, desperate for any other answer. "What do you want from us?"

"Nothing," he insisted casually, shaking the empty water bottle to remind her of their task. He turned toward the river again, walking away from her.

She thought about running, but even when she finally convinced herself to move, it was toward him. "Then why? Why did you kill everyone?"

"I didn't."

"You killed Megan," she pointed out quickly.

He stopped, and so did she, only an arm's reach behind him. He looked back, and she wondered if he was surprised that she knew. And then he huffed and went back to his path. "The camera." He shook his head to himself. "Megan was suspicious and paranoid."

"It's not paranoia if you're right."

"Of course, it is. If she had kept calm, she would still be alive." He let out a short laugh. "Well, she *might* be anyway. You've been killing each other right and left. Look at poor Maeko."

He walked around a tree, and her heart quickened, terrified that he might vanish only because she feared where he would reappear. She hurried to keep him in her sights, putting herself even closer to him when they finally came to the riverbank.

"What's your name?"

"Name?" He shook his head. "You humans love naming things. I don't have one. I don't need one. Names are for things that need to be remembered, things that die. Names are for humans and the things that they discover." He turned fully to look at her. "Zach liked naming things, and so did Julie."

Her face twisted with pain and anger, and she hated

the way his eyebrows lifted with interest. He leaned closer, head tipping to the side to study her expression.

"I know everything Zach knew," he continued, voice edged with curiosity. "I know how much you loved your sister and how much she loved you. I know how you got those scars." His arm came out, pointing two fingers down the length of her arm at the old scars above and below the bandages. "Funny, that nature would be so cruel to you when she did so much to shield you from me."

Val felt her skin prickle wherever his attention fell. Her scars burned when he pointed at them, raw, as though that shark's teeth were still buried in her skin. Her forehead scrunched at his words. He spoke of nature as though it were a person, a single decisive soul, and she feared that she would never be able to think of it any other way from then on.

Her gaze slid past him for a second to the river he had stopped at. He didn't stand close to it. Even if she tackled him now, they would only land on the bank. He couldn't cross. Julie had been right. He built that bridge of bones just as he'd built the dam of shoes and used the corpse of a jaguar to cross a stream.

"You're trapped." She shuddered at the thought because that made the island a prison and her a captive, too. "How long have you been here?" She pressed for another answer, fearing what would happen when their conversation ended.

"How long has it been since this land broke from the rest?" His lips tugged against the gleaming white of his teeth, twitching in a way she'd never seen a mouth twitch before. "I think nature must love your kind because she tries so hard to keep me from you." He grinned then, toothy and dark-eyed like a shark.

"But your kind can't resist me." He took a step closer, and Val didn't move, legs locked. The water bottle in her hand dented under the pressure of her fingers. "You come crawling," he continued, voice low. "You throw yourselves at me. Your families of hopefuls looking to build homes and grow crops. You're sick, sent to die out of sight. Your criminals, banished. Your soldiers, dedicated. They all come here, to me, and they all yield."

Val shivered, staring back. His eyes were nothing but pupils on bloodshot whites. "Then why are you still here?"

His teeth clicked, and she flinched. He was still smiling, and it chilled her to her core to stare at it so closely.

"I told you, flesh child. Nature loves you. She sinks your ships and drowns your weak, always sending me back here. I suspect she'd kill you all if it would save you from me."

Val shifted back, away from him, to hide her hand slipping into her pocket. Her fingers tugged the folded knife up until she could press it into her palm. "It doesn't sound like she loves us. It just sounds like she hates you."

He rolled his head to the side, looking at her curiously. "Are you going to kill me, human?" His mouth tugged at the sides when he spoke those words, a joke there that she didn't understand.

She thumbed the blade of the knife out. "I can't let you leave the island."

His smile grew, wider than she had ever imagined Calvin's mouth could. It was the single most sinister image she'd ever seen, pulling at half his face and making her stomach knot in terror that his cheeks might split and those teeth might snap at her. "Your sister said the same thing." It took her a moment to realize that while those teeth were still bared, he wasn't smiling anymore. "She's dead, Val." He dropped the water bottle he'd been carrying, and it rolled along the muddy riverbank. "They're coming to rescue the team. I don't need anyone to die, but I don't mind being the only one left to save either."

He took a step closer, and she took a step back. His arm bent behind him and came back with the large knife Calvin had taken from Lochner's body.

"Is Calvin still alive?" Val asked, shuffling another step away, moving to the side now as he followed, closing in on her. She could barely hear over her own pulse, her head throbbing with it.

He looked momentarily surprised, flicking the knife at his side like the tail of the big cat in the night. "Of course, in the most basic of ways." His arms spread as though to prove his point. "Walking, talking, breathing." He sniffled and rubbed the back of his wrist under his nose. It left a smear of blood, and he smiled at the timing. "Bleeding."

Her arm brushed against a tree as she stepped backward, the bark scraping her skin, reminding her how alive she was and how much a fight would hurt. She thought about Megan's body and how it had been thrown into the tree. What chance did she stand? "Why the nosebleeds? The eyes and ears, too. Zach was a mess near the end."

He lifted and dropped one shoulder in the laziest of shrugs. "You're weak," he explained bluntly.

The heel of her shoe hit a large rock, forcing her to an awkward stop. His body tensed, like a snake about to strike. She finally did the last thing she wanted to do, the last thing she ever thought she would—Val turned and ran. It was possibly the most terrifying moment of her life, with her back to him, unable to see how close he was, rushing along the riverbank. She remembered the footage from Megan's camera as she ran, that shadow of a man following. Val imagined it behind her now, not Calvin but that distortion of shapes, void of color.

She felt when he was close, heard his steps, and sensed her impending death. Her legs dropped out from under her just as the ground slanted toward the river and she let gravity pull her down below his swinging arm. She slid on her thigh all the way to the water, kicking at it to get to her feet and running into the river. The emerald green turned brown with silt when she stomped through it, churning up the bottom and trudging in until she was up to her waist. The cold current ran fast. She looked across it to the other side, but it was too far to swim. As soon as she lost her footing, the current would drag her away. Val whipped around to look back at the bank just as he came to it.

He froze as soon as the toes of his shoes reached the last edge of land, just before the water. His body leaned forward, too far for human balance, and those dark eyes stared back at her.

Val barked a mad laugh, still holding her water bottle and knife, arms up and water pushing at her side. "What now?" she shouted over the river, voice trembling with nerves. "You can't cross this one."

His lips curled with a snarl, his eyes boring into her with the will to make her return to shore, or maybe just drown herself. When she was sure he'd shout in anger, his features relaxed and his mouth pulled into a small, content smile. It sent chills down her spine.

Val turned around just in time to see a large crocodile breaking the surface, tail snapping to drive it forward at her. Its jaw opened, and she saw the white flesh between long teeth. She twisted to the side, sucking in air so hard her throat ached. That solid, rough body dragged across her hip and waist, spinning her in the water. She heard the jaws snap. Not a clicking of teeth but a solid clap, like two beams of wood coming together. She dropped down to sink beneath the murky water, ducking under a second crocodile and pushing at its belly to keep herself down while it propelled itself over where she'd been standing.

Lifting her knees from the muddy bottom of the river, Val let the current have her. It pulled her fast, sweeping her in a tumble through the murky dark, and she did nothing to fight it.

Chapter 22

The current spun her in the depths of the river before spitting her toward the surface again. She gasped for swallows of air as soon as she could, before being sucked down again. She went under four times before the river finally gave her up to the softer shallows. She kicked and clawed her way to the river bank, panting for air and looking around wildly. She kept one eye on the river for crocodiles and the other on the jungle for worse predators.

She'd lost her water bottle somewhere in the river but managed to keep hold of her knife. She waited in the shallow, muddy waters of the riverbank for Calvin to reappear. She waited until her breath evened out and her hair stopped dripping down her face. He didn't come. She'd been dragged far enough down river that she couldn't see the spot where they had been, but she could hear the ocean.

Pushing at her knees, she got up on her feet again. Her shirt clung to her skin, and her pants and shoes squeaked with water when she walked. It was tempting to go straight for the beach and wait for the rescue. It would be easier and quieter. She could stop walking. Stop running. And just wait.

She trudged through the trees upriver. There was nothing to wait for on the beach but death because death would be making his way down river with her husband and Poppy. She didn't put her knife away, not even when she started jogging through the jungle. A troop of howler monkeys studied her from the treetops. They didn't sound the alarm this time, bouncing on their branches and leaning over to watch her go. She wondered if they were captives here, too, trapped with a monster and nowhere to run.

She walked and jogged through the jungle in intervals, keeping an eye on the river to her right to make sure she didn't get lost. She had just started jogging again when she heard someone calling her name. It was Felix's voice, and it hit her with a wave of relief to know that he was still alive. She moved toward him, soon able to see him up ahead. His hands cupped to carry his voice when he shouted her name. Had Calvin told them that she'd washed away in the river? Or had he made up some other story? Perhaps she'd gone mad and run off like Megan?

Val saw Poppy, face tight with worry and eyes scanning the jungle in the wrong direction. And then, just past her, walked Calvin. Val ran faster, lips curling. He didn't even walk like Calvin, no swagger, just an ease of motion.

Felix saw her first, hands dropping from his mouth and her name gushing from his lips in relief. He started toward her, but she didn't move to meet him. She didn't leap into his arms and cling to the comfort he could offer. She ran past him, past Poppy, and jumped at the monster wearing Calvin's skin. He turned just as she came at him, and for one brief moment, he was surprised. His arms came up, maybe intending to push her away, but her arms and legs were already around him. His hands grabbed at her thighs and Felix shouted her name behind her now, no longer calling out for her but calling to her. She didn't listen.

With tears burning in her eyes, she grabbed a fistful of Calvin's sandy blond hair and jerked his head back. His eyes widened, and darkness stared up at her. She couldn't understand that expression. It wasn't Calvin's. It wasn't human. Her other arm came up above them both with that short knife held tight in her balled fist. Poppy screamed, but just as quickly as Val's arm shot up, it sank down. She felt his fingers convulse against her thighs when that blade cut into his neck. It stabbed down and vanished into his flesh, disappearing until she jerked the knife free. Red exploded up with the blade, bursting from the side of his neck to paint her skin and splatter the leafy greens all around them.

Before she could stab him again, Felix grabbed her by the waist and lifted her off of him. She didn't kick or scream or fight. She let him carry her away and watched Calvin drop to his knees. He grabbed at his neck, but the blood was too fast, slipping between his fingers. He coughed, and more red came up to paint his teeth and dribbled down his chin.

Poppy rushed to his side, falling to the ground and trying to help him hold in the blood that was so desperate to escape.

Val tried to move then, only to realize that Felix was still holding her up off the ground, her back to his chest and his eyes glued to the dying man. "What have you done?" he whispered in shock against her cheek.

"Get away from him!" Val shouted at Poppy, but she

didn't listen.

Calvin turned gray quickly, no longer breathing but choking on his own blood.

Poppy cried, shaking her head in confusion. "What do I do?" she shouted, repeating it twice before Calvin suddenly lurched forward.

His palms slapped the ground, abandoning their work at his neck, and his head flung back. The gash in the side of his throat split wider when his mouth gaped. A terrible sound rolled up from his chest, barreling out past those wide-open lips. His whole body convulsed as he vomited mouthfuls of dark blood; thick and congealed, it heaved from his throat and onto the ground. The sound kept coming, rolling out of him until it was near deafening. A roaring, rushing, gushing sound like wind and screams and drums all meshed together.

Poppy fell back, staring.

Felix slowly let go of Val, and she landed steadily on her feet.

When it was done, the jungle was quiet again as though nothing had happened, and Calvin's body lay face-down in the grass.

"What was that?" Felix asked, his voice low.

Val walked the short distance to Calvin's body and turned him over carefully. She closed his eyes and then stood up again, looking down at him. She told herself that the monster killed him, but it was her hand that grew sticky with his cooling blood. "Julie was right."

Poppy cried, shaking her head and scrambling to her feet and away from Val. "Y-you killed him!" She pushed the heels of her palms against her temples. "What the fuck, Val? You killed him!"

"He wasn't him," she said it and cringed because it

sounded like madness in her mouth the same way it had in Julie's.

Felix came closer, putting himself in the space between the two women. "Something came out of him," he said, trying to think this through, probably trying to find an answer that could make sense and not make his wife a murderer.

"Yeah, a lot of blood!" Poppy shouted.

Val sucked an angry breath through her clenched teeth. "You're going to pretend you didn't see that? Didn't hear that?"

"I didn't!" she lied, desperate not to know. She shook her head hard, taking two more steps back. "You killed him. You're a murderer. You—" She stopped suddenly, body leaning forward as though something struck her from behind. Her eyes closed tight and her whole face wrinkled with a deep cringe.

Felix started to move closer, but Val reached out to grab his arm, pulling him back.

Poppy's eyes opened suddenly. Her shoulders lifted with a deep breath, and then her whole body relaxed. Those dark eyes cut across Felix to land squarely on Val.

Poppy smiled. "Did you think that would work?"

"What?" Felix asked, confused.

Val let out a small curse and tightened her grip on her knife, but before she could move, Poppy waggled a finger in her direction. "Ah-ah. Be careful, flesh bag. You're running out of bodies. Three left. If you ruin this one, I might take yours next." Her mouth pulled into a vicious grin, the same one Val had seen on Calvin.

Felix recoiled a step and cursed under his breath in Spanish. It wasn't Poppy. It wasn't her smile or her stance or her words.

"Or maybe I'll take him before I take you," the creature suggested, jutting a chin in Felix's direction. "Maybe I'll make you kill him to save yourself and then wear your skin when I get off this island."

The knife felt heavy in her hand.

"Drop it. You don't need it," Death said. "I'm giving you a last chance. Your only chance. You want to get off this island? You want to save yourself? Fine. Take me with you and I will let you live out your little lives in peace." Her mouth twitched, as though trying not to laugh. "Whatever peace you can find between the sharks and the leeches, that is." Poppy folded her arms across her chest, infinitely patient. "I will spare you, and it will cost you nothing."

Val laughed, short and miserable. A few tears rolled down her cheeks, but she dropped the knife. Nothing. The price was already so high.

"Good choice, flesh bag," Poppy said before turning and walking through the trees, expectant that they would follow.

For a few seconds, they didn't, minds reeling in search of an alternative, but Poppy had the beacon, and the beach would be their only chance of leaving Isla de los Perdidos. Val reached out and grabbed onto Felix's hand. She didn't have to look to find it, and she didn't have to pull for him to follow.

They were going to walk Death to the beach.

Chapter 23

Poppy led the way. It seemed right. She would know the island best.

Felix tried to get the same answers Val had fished for with Calvin. He wanted a name to call the creature other than Poppy, because of all the things it was, it was no longer her. She wouldn't give a name, once again contemptuous at the suggestion that she even had one. He wanted to know why and how. She didn't complain about the questions, but she answered with monotone disinterest, as though it was the hundredth time. Val wondered if it was, or if it was the thousandth. How many people had taken a walk through this jungle with this monster? It would always be the same questions, wouldn't it? What are you? Why are you doing this to us? What do you want?

"Is Poppy still in there?" Felix asked quietly, studying the creature they followed.

Poppy turned her head to look at them over her shoulder. "What do you mean?" she asked, one hand tapping at her chest over her heart. "This is Poppy."

"No." Felix swallowed. "Her soul. Is she still alive? If

you left her body now, would she be okay?"

Poppy laughed, but it was a hollow sound, void of joy. "No. When I leave this body, it will be dead."

Val felt Felix's shoulders sag and held his hand tighter to keep him moving at her side. She couldn't do this without him.

"But I know everything Poppy knew. I know everything she did, heard, felt, saw, and thought." She turned around and walked backward, never losing a step, to look at her two captives. "Did you have any questions for her? Unresolved issues?" Her eye twinkled and her smile twisted wider when she looked at Felix. "Feelings?"

Felix glared back at the body of his friend. It wasn't her, and they knew that now more than ever.

"*She* had feelings," Poppy continued, winking at Felix before looking at Val. "Did you know?"

"Know what?" Val baited.

"About that night on the beach, with the bonfire."

"Stop it," Felix hissed.

"She had such a crush on you," Poppy told Felix, nibbling her lip. "She was so conflicted because she was friends with Val. You were family to her, but oh how she wanted you to be more. The things she thought about. The things she wanted to do to you and have you do to her—"

"So?" Val interrupted. "If thinking was cheating, we'd all be in a lot of trouble." She smiled a little, too tired and raw to feel scared of this creature anymore. They were going to die today, so why spend it shaking and crying? "You were in Calvin's head, too, weren't you? Are you telling me that he never thought about Felix?" She let her smile grow to a near laugh. "He's hot. Who doesn't think about messing him up a little?"

Felix looked at her, surprised. If he weren't so anxious

and freaked out, he would have been amused.

"So true," Poppy agreed, still walking backward. She didn't have to look over her shoulder to navigate, avoiding trees and roots easily. "But Poppy did more than think about Felix." She grinned wider when Val's smile dwindled.

Felix squeezed her hand, but Val didn't squeeze back. She stared ahead at Poppy. "Liar."

Poppy lifted a hand to cross her heart with a long finger. "Never, my dear flesh bag. Never."

Val hissed through her teeth. "You lied when you pretended to be our friends. You lied when you wore their skin and turned us on each other."

Poppy shrugged. "That was when we were playing. Now you know, and the time for pretending is over. I told you, you should have stuck with the lies. You could have died not knowing how Poppy fucked your husband."

"Wow." Felix shook his head, eyes wide. "I never had sex with Poppy."

Poppy raised an eyebrow. "Are you going to be the liar now?" She giggled. "The beach was warm that night, the bonfire lighting up the party, but we were in the water, in the dark, under the moonlight."

"Felix..." Val murmured his name in place of a thousand questions.

He squeezed her hand tighter. "No."

"They were playing in the water. He picked her up in his arms and carried her to the beach. She was overcome by lust, took his face in her hands, and kissed him." Poppy continued, sidestepping a tree. The ground turned to sand, lumpy and rough with twigs and leaves. They could hear the waves rolling against the beach, the trees growing sparse and the world brighter and brighter with midday sun.

"Admit that you cheated," Poppy implored. "It might be your last chance, and humans do love to confess before they die."

Val looked to her husband at her side and watched him swallow hard, his eyes glassy. He shook his head slowly. "It was just a kiss, Val. She was drunk. She was so embarrassed afterward."

"That's not how I remember it," Poppy continued to prod.

Val sucked down a breath and jerked her hand free of his, shoving at his chest. "Are you kidding? I remember that party!" He reached for her, desperate to explain, but she smacked his hand away. Poppy laughed, delighted, and Val stomped forward, past her to get away from Felix.

She walked out past the last trees and onto the beach, taking a handful more strides toward the bright blue surf before turning back to shout at him. "I can't believe you! All those years you said I was being paranoid!"

Poppy grinned wide, following her now. "Do you want to know more?" she offered. "How he kissed her? What they did after, on the beach, so close to where you were laughing with friends?" She rolled her head to the side to look at Felix. He was closing that space between himself and his wife, arms out and mouth working with pleas to convince Val of his fidelity and love.

The creature in Poppy never saw it coming.

Val grabbed her arms from behind just as Felix reached them. Before Poppy could turn on Val, Felix scooped up her legs. They never spoke of their intentions. It was a plan in the most primal of designs. They lifted her up between them and kept moving, right out into the surf. The shape of a rescue boat bobbed far out on the horizon. So close, but not close enough.

Poppy shouted and arched, that scream turning wrath-
ful when she saw the water rolling across the sand beneath her. "No! What are you doing? I'll come back!"

"I don't care," Val hissed, the waves splashing up to
hit her hips when they moved deeper.

"But he betrayed you! He—"

"You might have Poppy's memories to play with, but
you don't have mine," Val said. "It was a kiss and she
was drunk and he told me that night."

"I didn't tell Poppy that Val knew because she was
already embarrassed," Felix explained simply.

Poppy writhed between them, arching up to try to stay
out of the water. "You'll never make it off this island! You'll
die, and I'll use your bones for my bridge!"

Val stopped and looked at Felix.

They dropped Poppy. She fell like a stone, violent bubbles gushing up from her mouth. They stood there in the
surf with her between them until she floated up at last.
Her eyes were open, and blood rolled like thick tears down
her temples and into her ears.

Felix took a deep breath, and Val reached out to gently
close her eyes.

The waves pushed at them, trying to pull Poppy's body
away, but for long minutes they held on to her.

"I can't put her back on the island," Val finally admitted.

Felix nodded. "She liked the ocean," he agreed, and together, when the water was pulling back, they let her go.
She vanished into the sea, and they were left alone.

"We can't go back to shore," Felix said what she was
thinking.

She looked back at the island, and there, in the trees,
stood a small deer, body rigid and head lifted high to watch

them with large dark eyes. Was it the monster or just another animal trapped in that jungle?

"What do we do?" Felix asked, reaching out in the water to touch her hand.

Val looked up at him. He was watching the sea. The larger boat on the horizon had dropped a dingy that was motoring toward the island. "If they come here..." Felix began, voice full of dread.

She nodded, watching the smaller boat make its way toward the reef and then looking at the stretch of water between them and that coral barrier built on the wreckage of ships. Fins cut the surface every now and then, marking the presence of the massive fish swarming between.

"We won't make it," Val said, remembering what Julie had said. The animals were going to make sure they didn't get off the island.

"Always the optimist," Felix muttered with a smirk before he sighed and nodded. He squeezed her hand. "On the island or in the water?"

His voice was soft, but she could hear the gentle smile of his lips around his words. She looked up at him once more. He was asking where she wanted to die, and Val knew he would be there with her, whatever choice she made. She smiled back, exhausted, and then looked out at the ocean. If they didn't swim out to meet the dingy, the rescue team would have to send people ashore to get them. A helicopter moved overhead, the sound of propellers competing with waves.

Val pulled her shirt off over her head and tossed it away before reaching down and squirming out of her pants and shoes. "Let's at least try to survive," she decided.

Felix smiled at the challenge and followed suit, stripping down to his underwear. He followed her out into the surf. She ducked under one wave and started swimming. Underwater, she could see the clear blue stretch of ocean speckled with large shadows. They swam hard but close to one another, always pushing forward.

A tiger shark bumped against her side, and for a moment, it looked at her, considering her before pushing past. Her nerves jumped and air pushed from her lungs before she came up to take another gulp. All she could do was keep swimming, keep kicking. The closer they came to the dingy, the more afraid she was that they wouldn't make it. Every time her head came up, she looked to the side to make sure that Felix was still there, still swimming, still alive.

She started crying when she heard the voices of the rescue team calling out to them. The worst moment was when she reached the small rubber boat and a hand reached over the edge to grab her arms. When she was half out of the water, she was sure that a shark would come up to grab her and take her back. She landed on the floor of the dingy, people bustling around her, asking questions in Spanish. She opened her mouth to answer but could only gasp for air, her vision blurred, the sky too bright and too blue.

They asked again where the rest of the crew was, and before she lost consciousness, she heard Felix answer. Everyone else was dead. Twelve people had gone out to Isla de los Perdidos, and only two had come back.

Chapter 24

Val sat in the dark jungle. It was loud, and she was never alone. Even without the sun, it was hot. Her skin sticky, and every breath she drew miserably warm.

Julie sat across from her, legs folded and one of those small red deer in her lap. She petted it like a cat, smiling down at it.

Val felt afraid, staring at her sister's hands passing over that speckled fur. She wanted to move but couldn't. She wanted to speak but could only draw slow, steady breaths.

Julie looked up and smiled, blood tears rolling down her cheeks unnoticed. "You'll never leave the island," she said sweetly. "But I'll be here with you. Always."

Val jolted awake, eyes opening and vision a blur of colors and shapes. She sucked down large gulps of air, remembering the ocean and the dingy. The air didn't smell or taste like the sea. It smelt chemical and filtered. A firm hand pressed against her shoulder, and she stared up at the shape of a man, blurry and slowly coming into focus.

"Wow. Calm down," Felix urged, thumb rubbing her collarbone while his other hand found her cheek. She blinked up at him, nodding slowly, and he smiled in relief. He wore a clean shirt and cotton pants. Hospital clothing. "We're on the mainland," he assured, and she looked around at the room to confirm it.

The tile and curtains were all in muted colors. Her bed was framed in plastic with thin blankets tucked in around her legs. Raindrops speckled the window, each glowing with the streetlights and signs outside in the night.

"You've been in and out of consciousness since the boat picked us up. They said it was exhaustion and an infection from the bite," Felix continued. Val looked at her arm; it had been rewrapped in bright white gauze. "They pumped you with a bunch of antibiotics and started you on rabies treatments just in case." He touched her hair, pushing it away from her face. "How are you feeling?"

She swallowed hard, her mouth dry. A tube snaked from her arm to a bag of what looked like water dangling from a metal stand. "Bad," she managed before flopping back onto the bed and taking a few slow breaths.

Felix nodded, kissing her forehead. "I'll get you some water." He left her bedside and started for the door, stopping halfway out of it to look back at her. "Hey," he called, and she looked back. He smiled just a little. "You saved me."

Val smiled back and shrugged. "I said I would." She held up her thin smile until he had gone and then let the gesture slip away. She had saved him and herself but no one else. Julie was dead. Everyone was dead.

The soft tapping of knuckles against her doorframe had her turning her head back to it, expecting to see Felix again.

Henry stood there, leaning against the open door and smiling. He didn't look well. Gray and tired, with heavy bags under his bloodshot eyes. But he was smiling all the same, like a wolf in a field of fat sheep.

"No," Val exhaled, her pulse quickening and the machine to the right beeping as it took note. She sat up slowly, blinking and expecting him to disappear.

He didn't.

"I had to fake a broken leg on that beach, but they airlifted me out," he explained, voice soft to respect the quiet of the sleepy hospital. "How your kind has multiplied and conquered the world. So many inventions to trump nature. Beautiful."

She shook in her bed, staring at him. There was no river to dump him in now. No ocean to drag him into the surf of. Nowhere to hide.

His smile changed, impossible to grow any larger. "It wouldn't work, flesh bag," he said, reading any hope of a plan in her eyes. "I'm off the island, and there is no sending me back. But I'm not here to kill you," he promised, pulling a red handkerchief from his jacket pocket and dabbing the blood from his ears. "I told you, if I got off the island I would not end your life or Felix's." He looked at the handkerchief and sighed, shaking it out. "It was white yesterday," he noted. "How can your kind be so weak but so clever? They flew me off the island in a funny, little bird, metal with a spinning top. Brilliant." He dropped the handkerchief and leaned toward Val. She held her breath, terrified that he might take a step closer or lunge for her. But he didn't. "I came to warn you."

She swallowed, but her mouth was still dry. "Warn me?" The words ground out, and he laughed a little at her struggle.

"I told you before." He looked up, shoving the bloody handkerchief back into his pocket. "Nature loves you, though I cannot imagine why. She will do all she can to save you from me."

A nurse walked by just then, stopping when she noticed Henry. She began to explain in Spanish that it wasn't visiting hours and if he wasn't family he would have to leave. Henry turned toward her and smiled before grabbing onto her shoulders. She gasped in shock, but before she could scream, he opened his mouth wide, jaw popping, and let loose that horrible sound. It came gushing out of him, rattling the window in its frame and making Val's stomach churn and vision sway. Blood rolled from his eyes and ears and mouth in thick, black globs. The nurse inhaled sharply, eyes glazing over, and he let go.

Henry's corpse collapsed into a pile on the floor and the short nurse with her soft body and braided black hair took a deep breath all the way down to her toes and then relaxed.

Val sat breathlessly on the bed, staring at the woman.

The nurse looked back at her, a small smile on her round lips. She winked and then walked away.

Minutes rolled by, and Val could only sit there, staring at the body in her doorway. Another nurse let out a shout when he saw the fallen man, rushing over to check on Henry, but it was too late. Chaos gathered in her doorway, voices shouting about disease and quarantine, examining his bleeding eyes and ears.

They didn't quiet until the rumbling below grew so loud that they couldn't ignore it. The hospital shook, and new screams came from all directions. Val looked out her window to see the earthquake rocking the city, car alarms sounding and lights going out. Smoke gushed into the air and sirens flared to life as buildings swayed.

She remembered his words, spoken from Calvin's mouth by the river.

"Nature loves you. I suspect she'd kill you all if it would save you from me."

From her window, she saw the ground split open and whole buildings sink away from the skyline.

And then the lights of the hospital went out.

ABOUT THE AUTHOR

Cheryl Low might be a primeval entity, born from the darkness of the universe and vacationing on a forgotten island where she eats coconuts and the souls of stranded sailors.

…Or she might be a human with a deep love of horror and absolutely no interest in coconuts.

Find out for yourself by following her on social media @cherylwlow or check out her webpage, CherylLow.com.

The answer could surprise you!

But it probably won't.

Press
Presents

For more apocalyptic fiction, check out *The Demon Guardian* by Neil Davies.

Made in the USA
Middletown, DE
24 November 2019